The Enchantresses

By the same author

THE THREE DAMOSELS

The Enchantresses

VERA CHAPMAN

VICTOR GOLLANCZ
LONDON

First published in Great Britain 1998
by Victor Gollancz
An imprint of the Cassell Group
Wellington House, 125 Strand, London, WC2R OBB

A catalogue record for this book is
available from the British Library.

ISBN 0 575 06524 9

Typeset by SetSystems Ltd, Saffron Walden, Essex
Printed in Great Britain by
St Edmundsbury Press Ltd, Bury St Edmunds, Suffolk

98 99 5 4 3 2 1

CONTENTS

Part I: Before the King *page* 7

1. The Daughters 9
2. Little Witches 17
3. Greater Witches 26
4. Wizard Schoolmaster 33
5. Knight Errant 43
6. Belle Dame Sans Merci 56

Part II: The King That Shall Be 67

1. Something Brewing 69
2. Noble Guest 75
3. Terms of Peace 82
4. Who Goes There? 92
5. Child of the Storm 101
6. The Lady of the Lake 112
7. Mischief Afoot 123

Part III: The King Hereafter 135

1. A Sword for Arthur 137
2. Arthur the King 153
3. The Wonderful Ship 162
4. The Treachery of Morgan 173
5. The Stones of Broceliande 200
6. The Door Without a Key 210
7. So Passes Arthur 218

PART I

Before the King

1. The Daughters

'Congratulations, madame,' said the midwife. 'You have three lovely daughters.'

'Two,' said the Duchess, faintly.

'Three, I assure you, madame.'

'I should know,' said the Duchess, feebly moving her head on the fine down pillow. 'I am quite sure it was only two.'

The midwife pulled herself up to her full height and put on her best no-nonsense expression. 'Madame, you were in great pain and could hardly know what was happening. You were out of your mind for a time, I am sure.' She paused as she watched the Duchess's expression and then spoke again in a softer, more caring voice. 'You know, we feared for your life. But thank God, all is well. And here . . .' she stood back from the bed and, with a wave of her arm like the start of a cabaret, added, '. . . are your three lovely daughters.'

Three nurses approached the bedside, each carrying a white-swaddled bundle. Ygraine, Duchess of Cornwall, lifted her head a little and viewed them. Three downy heads – one yellow like a chicken, one with a tinge of red, one black. The eyes of both the blonde one and the red one were of the watery blue common to all newborn babies, but the third, the black-haired one, had eyes of an intense and startling blackness – shining, glossy and moist, like the berries of belladonna, the deadly nightshade.

'They must be christened,' said the Duchess in a voice of sudden apprehension.

'Madame,' said the midwife in her most reassuring tone, 'I have christened them already, at the earliest possible moment. We thought it was as well, for triplets are often weak and not likely to survive. So I christened them myself, and it only needs now for the priest to receive them.'

'*You* christened them?' Ygraine retorted with as much strength as she could muster. 'But they look healthy enough to me. What names did you give them?'

'Names you chose yourself, madame. Maybe you do not remember in your pain and torment and fever. But for a moment your mind was clear enough. You named them Morgan, Morgause and Vivian.'

The Duchess passed her long white hand over her brow.

'No, I . . . I don't remember. But I suppose it is all right . . . Morgan, Morgause and Vivian.' She repeated the names to herself reflectively. It was all very puzzling. Then as if the names were an incantation she found herself drowsing and could bring her mind to bear on it no longer. She could only sleep.

One thing the midwife did not tell her was that she had christened only two of the babies.

*

The place where the triplets grew up was wild and strange: a rocky peninsula where stood a fierce and formidable castle, rising sheer out of the waves. It looked vast, massive, imposing. Terraces and crags led up out of the deep water to a distance where the rocky foundation was secure from falling back into the sea – and there arose a frowning wall, enclosing the space within against enemies. And within that, secure from all human foes, rose the motte and bailey of the castle of Tintagel. Only a narrow causeway, with angry waves thundering on either side, joined it to the mainland. From the castle the iron cliffs stretched away on either side, ancient and hostile. There was one great echoing arch of stone, as vast and empty as the roof of a church, under which the coloured pebbles sometimes lay quiet, whispering to the waves, or sometimes chattered in anger at the huge crashing breakers that thundered into the cave like a battling army.

Such was the home of the three little daughters of Ygraine, the beautiful Duchess of Cornwall, and of Gorlais, the Duke. High on one wall of the castle were windows made of little panes of thin glass which could never be opened. Through the opaqueness and grime of centuries the little girls could look out on the tempestuous sea. Within this hall, its high stone walls were covered with tapestries which swayed and whispered in the draughts, so that the lords and ladies stiffly pictured there seemed to be stirring and beckoning. In the middle of the room stood the great bed where the three princesses slept together, and at its foot was set a brazier of charcoal or clear-burning wood. The head nurse (and midwife) was always cautioning the subordinate nurses not to knock the brazier and upset it, for it was very far from safe, and the room was strewn with dry but sweet-smelling rushes and camomile. But what else could one do for warmth? Every night the serving-men would carry the brazier out, lest the vapours from the charcoal choke them all in their sleep, and then the three little girls had to huddle together in the big bed to keep warm, amidst the sounds of the shifting tapestries, the crashing waves and the keening gulls. It was a world of smoke and shadow and distant thunder.

The great chamber where the Duke and Duchess slept had a stone chimney and a fire that burned all night. The big hall below, which took up most of the living space of the castle, had a hearth in the middle, with a smoke-hole above, where the smoke from the vast log fire escaped and billowed above the turrets amongst the flags and pennants that signified that the Duke was at home. Here the house-carls and the men-at-arms slept around the fire with the dogs. It was a rough place and the princesses did not go there. But the solar, which was built above one end of the great hall, and partitioned by a small winding stone staircase and a solid door, was cosy and civilized. It had a casement window that opened on to a small courtyard within, where the high walls to the north, east and west kept the cold winds out and the sun came in at the south and filled it with sunshine, like a well with water. Here, on fine days, the casement could be set open, and under it were flowers and sweet herbs, apple trees, pears and medlars, and a hive of bees. The solar itself had a wooden floor under fresh rushes, covered with a carpet, while the wall was lined with the best tapestries. The niches were filled with flowers and scented sachets. Even on a stormy day one could always be comfortable in the solar, with a brazier that burned perfume, thick rugs on the floor, comfortable chairs and sofas, and always the castle cats and dogs to pet and fondle.

Each of the three little girls had a nurse to herself, who breast-fed her in infancy, and took careful charge of her as she grew. And over them was the head nurse, a tall, dark woman, called Olwen La Nourrice, who spoke little but commanded obedience. Though she retained the title of La Nourrice, her function as nurse was only supervisory. The three younger nurses were nonentities compared with her, and the girls stood more in awe of her than of their mother or even their father. Their mother was beautiful and glamorous but rather remote; their father, dark-haired and long-faced, was fully absorbed in his hunting and fighting.

There was always fighting. So long as the girls remained in the castle, they were safe; but out on the mainland there was always battle to be done. Day after day the Duke would ride out across the causeway with a hundred men or so, leaving another hundred to garrison the castle. The Duchess always looked pale and anxious when he went. Sometimes he was away for weeks and, when he returned, not all of his men came with him. The whys and wherefores of all this were puzzling to the little girls, but Gwen, Vivian's nurse, explained to them that away beyond the cliffs were fields of corn and barley, pastures where cattle and sheep grazed, and woods where deer, partridges and hares could be caught, and without all that there would be no food in the castle. But there were bad men who wanted to take some of the fields and woods away from the Duke. And the name that was whispered with fear most often was that of Uther Pendragon.

The little girls grew up as little girls do, thriving and maturing quite uniformly until the day when differences began to show between them. Morgause was blonde, roly-poly and dimpled, and in babyhood quite the prettiest of the three, with her blue wide-opened eyes and her yellow curls, like a baby doll. But she was greedy and lazy and soon showed a tendency to plumpness. She was forever eating, and when they could get sweetstuff, she would snatch it from the others (with an almost unconscious smirk) and gorge on it. Vivian, whose red hair and green eyes were like her mother's, was livelier and quicker in her movements, not quite as tall as the others, and light on her feet. But Morgan – well, Ygraine had to suppose that she took after some grandparent of Gorlais for, though he was dark, this child was much darker. Though white of skin, to be sure, her hair was so black and her brows and eyes so dark as to make her the exact opposite of her sisters. But charming she certainly was, with her coal-black curls, her sensuous red mouth and her eyes like shining blackberries in the dew. And she was changeable of temperament: sometimes wildly, impishly mirthful, sometimes withdrawn and remote, sitting by herself and thinking her own thoughts, mischievous and strange.

When they were all quite little, an odd thing happened. During the winter days they all spent hours around the brazier, each little princess on her own nurse's lap, and Olwen La Nourrice in the middle, spinning with distaff and spindle, and sometimes telling them long stories. Olwen's big black and white cat sat composedly by her side on a cushion specially kept for her, sometimes drowsing with shut eyes, sometimes staring. And Morgan would stare back. Morgan's own nurse, Lissa, could not look directly into her face, but Vivian's nurse, Gwen, sitting opposite her, could. Suddenly Gwen gave a shriek and threw her hands before her, nearly letting Vivian fall. She clutched her with one hand, while making the sign of the cross with the other, and she gibbered, 'The Lord between us and all harm!' whilst she looked backwards and forwards from Morgan to the cat and the cat to Morgan.

'Gwen, what's the matter?' asked Olwen severely. 'Why are you upsetting us all? You look like you've seen a ghost. Don't be a fool, girl.'

Gwen struggled to recover her composure, flinching slightly from Olwen's admonition. 'Oh, it's nothing, Dame Olwen. I'll tell you later.'

And later she told her. 'As I looked at the little Lady Morgan, and she looked at the cat, her face began to change, as God sees me, I swear it! Her face became like the cat's – pointed chin, little flat nose, eyes round and green – yes, greener than Lady Vivian's, and slit too, like the cat's. If she'd opened her mouth I swear I'd've seen little sharp teeth—'

'Oh nonsense, girl,' Olwen replied, brusquely. 'Sheer imagination. It's easy enough to imagine such things. Don't think about it any more.'

And that was before the children could speak. Gwen said nothing, but sometimes she caught Morgan looking intently towards Morgause and, in a few minutes, Gwen would be wondering at the astonishing family likeness. Why, Morgan's eyes were blue, not black, and her hair was yellow in the light, and she was putting on weight . . . Then something broke Morgan's concentration and the illusory resemblance was gone. Or she would, another time, seem to become like Vivian: red hair, green eyes and all. And one day, being near a mirror, Vivian and Morgan looked at their reflections together, and Gwen, looking over their shoulders, saw two Morgans. Gwen found it all rather upsetting, but the other two nurses did not seem to notice – at first – and Dame Olwen severely repressed all comments and questions.

The three girls, of course, understood each other long before speech, and kept a giggling conspiracy against the world. As they grew bigger, it seemed that Morgan had shared with them her special skill in taking on the face and even the shape of anyone they wished. They began to play a game of 'Who shall we be?' The other two nurses were finally convinced something odd was going on when one day, coming into the tower room with the midday dinner on a tray, they found three Vivians sitting waiting for them. The three trays crashed to the ground. Since the three dinners were lost, the girls came to an agreement that it might be better not to play that trick at meal times. But at other times, such as when they were required to attend chapel, or to be groomed, the nurses would find two Vivians and one Morgan, or two Morgauses, and go running round looking for the missing one, only to find her sitting with the rest and waiting. The nurses became more and more worried, but Dame Olwen brushed it aside as if there was nothing unusual in it. Above all, she would not have a word said to the Duke or Duchess. And the girls never played their tricks when their parents were there.

2. Little Witches

In all these tricks it was Morgan who was the ringleader, the instigator of all the mischief. Although Olwen seemed to know this, she indulged her all the time. Vivian and Morgause sometimes complained that Olwen spoiled Morgan and let her get away with things that they were not allowed to do, but as this was the way things always had been they suffered it, and followed Morgan's lead. She repaid them for abetting her mischief: Vivian with kisses and caresses, Morgause with stolen sweets.

Morgause followed Morgan implicitly, but Vivian was more cautious. Morgan had a streak of cruelty that showed itself very early – teasing and tormenting the dogs, beating them; catching insects and pulling off their limbs as they struggled. Morgause would join in with Morgan, laughing when she laughed, but Vivian would run away. There was a time when, ranging the rough ground outside the walls, they found a rabbit in a snare. Morgan stood over it, clapping her hands and hissing, laughing to see the poor creature struggling in its terror and choking itself on the noose. Morgause stood by her side applauding, but Vivian cried out and quickly unpegged the noose and let the rabbit free. Morgan shrugged her shoulders and called Vivian silly. But Morgause stamped her feet, calling Vivian a spoil-sport and slapping her face. Vivian could only run away and cry, but at least the rabbit had escaped.

They were now seven years old.

In the fine days of summer they would walk along the stony path outside the wall and look down on the sea, and the seals would come up and hitch their shoulders upon the rocks, and look at the girls with their big wet eyes. Vivian felt rather glad that the water's edge was too far away from the path for Morgan to get to the seals and torment them, though one day she did see Morgan sit on a rock and concentrate on a seal till her face was a seal's face and the shape of her body began dimly to take on a seal's sleekness. She was seized with dread about what Morgan would do next.

'Oh Morgan, don't do it,' she pleaded.

'Don't do what, silly?'

'Don't turn into a seal. You'll get into the water with them and swim away, and we'll never ever see you again.'

'Oh you *are* silly, Vivian. Of course I won't.' Though as she spoke, her face still seemed to have the rounded outlines of a seal's face, the pouched cheeks, the dog-like mouth and the bristly whiskers round the muzzle. 'I don't like fish all that much,' she added in a lighter tone, which made Vivian smile with an uncertain hesitancy. Morgan passed a hand over her face and wiped away the last vestige of the illusion, but she kept her eyes fast fixed on Vivian. 'Would you like me to make you into a seal?'

'Oh no, Morgan, no, please don't.'

'For a couple of pins, I would.'

And suddenly Vivian, by now really afraid of what Morgan might do to her, found that she could shape-change. In her moment of fright she transformed into one of a nearby clump of sapling willows. Morgan had briefly looked away and did not see the change. When she looked round for her and could not see her, she believed Vivian had run away. Losing interest, she went after Morgause, back to the castle. Only then did Vivian resume her own shape and follow her sisters at a distance up the winding path.

The next day they were down by the water again. It was a grey and overcast day, the surface of the sea ruffled and broken, the waves high on the exposed side of the peninsula, but beating more calmly where the shore was sheltered. As they came near the water they heard the sound of music and there, on the rock where they usually saw the seals, were half-a-dozen strange forms, partly in the water. Their heads and shoulders were human, gleaming dark grey in colour, with long green hair, but their bodies, human to the loins, descended into fish tails. One of them, propped against a large stone, was playing a harp, and a strange plaintive singing came from the others. The girls gave a gasp of astonishment, and then Morgan laughed.

'Hail to you,' she called.

The sea-people dragged themselves out of the water as far as they could, off the flat rock and up the rough shingle. They hailed Morgan, not in words, but in a kind of song.

'Come nearer,' she called.

They tried to struggle nearer. The foremost one, like a rather fat old man, wheezed and coughed. By his side was one like a grey-haired old lady, who slipped back into the water.

'Oh, try harder!' Morgan mocked them. 'You're lazy and fat.'

The sea-people pushed themselves and each other as far up the pebbly slope as they could.

'Oh poor things, let them alone,' said Vivian.

'Not a bit of it. They're fat and lazy. I know all about them. No, you silly merrows, you're eating too much. I shall have to tell the fish to keep out of your way.'

The mer-people moaned in their musical language. They seemed to be afraid of Morgan. Some of them had tears spilling over their cheeks, like seals. They tried to shuffle their way up the shingle, the small, sharp pebbles running backwards along the grain of their scales. Then Morgause picked up a handful of pebbles and began to take shots at them. As she hit them they shrieked, and this seemed to break the spell Morgan held over them. They turned and plunged back into the water, submerged and disappeared. All, that is, except one. In its panic to escape Morgause's stones it had slipped on the rocks and caught its arm in a fissure. It shouted in pain, its cries ululating eerily across the water. Morgause and Morgan laughed, but Vivian grimaced at its pain. She called out to it and stepped cautiously over the rocks towards the screaming creature.

The creature panicked more at Vivian's approach, but as she drew near, she stopped and spoke in soft, kind tones. She had not realized the size of the merrow from the shore. Close up it was bigger than a man. Strong muscles rippled in its arms, and Vivian was only too aware how strong its tail was. But as Morgan had ridiculed, the creatures had also run to flab, and the merrow's stomach bulged.

'Do not be afraid.' Vivian spoke soothingly. 'I want to help you.'

Although the fear remained in the creature's eyes, it ceased its thrashing. Slowly Vivian moved forward. Suddenly her mind was blasted with the creature's fear and pain. It momentarily knocked Vivian backward, but she instinctively responded. Although she had shared thoughts with her sisters, she had never tried projecting them to another before. But, through its own agony, the creature had opened a channel and Vivian responded. Her benign, gentle thoughts immediately relaxed the merrow. Carefully she reached down to where the arm was trapped in the rocks, all the time sending calming messages. She could see that in its panic the creature had broken its arm. Vivian had some healing powers, but had not yet developed them or used them to any significant degree. And she had only used them on herself, to relieve the sting of bruises or cuts. She might, however, be able to numb the pain.

She touched the arm and projected a soothing balm in her thoughts. She could sense that this was having an effect: the pain was reducing, the arm becoming anaesthetized. Gradually she eased it out of the rock. At first it was stiff and the creature reacted to a sharp return of the pain, but Vivian countered the shock, and with a quick jerk released the arm – but she did not let go. She ran her hand soothingly over the badly twisted limb, focusing her mind, trying desperately to knit the splintered bone and torn flesh back into place.

She had no real idea how well she was succeeding. She

knew only that the creature's pain was receding. The panic faded from its face. Its eyes became calmer, almost friendly. For a moment Vivian wondered whether this was the first kind act the creature had ever experienced.

Finally she let go and the merrow's instinct took over. Released, it immediately slithered back down the rocks to the sea, holding its broken arm aloft. Once in the sea it moved quickly, the injury seemingly no impediment. It dived beneath the waves, and Vivian thought it was gone, but then briefly it resurfaced and looked back towards her. In that moment a feeling of warmth and friendliness came over Vivian, and she smiled. The creature had thanked her.

As Vivian made her way back to the shore she was conscious of Morgan and Morgause scowling at her, but she ignored them, and made her way back to the castle.

When they were eight years old there was a change. It was early May and they had been sent to spend the summer on the mainland, in a farmhouse away on the other side of Cornwall, in the mild valleys and lush coombs of Roseland, where the warm current in the sea made everything tepid and steamy, and the trees and shrubs and flowers grew into a strange paradise. They had never seen woods before, or green lanes, or soft, grassy meadows. It was all enchantment to them. And they discovered new playfellows.

It was Vivian who saw them first, in a wood full of bluebells. Hosts of little people, green and blue, interpenetrating the massed flowers, moving weightlessly like insects, their delicate pale-green limbs waving in an incessant dancing motion. She cried out with delight and knelt down to take a closer look. Morgause did the same, and the little people clustered round them, touching their clothes, their hands, even their faces. But Morgan stood aloof, laughing soundlessly and not very pleasantly. Morgause turned to her with one of the sprites on her hand.

'Look, Morgan, aren't they sweet?'

Morgan stretched out her left hand, palm upwards, and with her right hand beckoned to the sprite. It came unwillingly and with slow steps on to her hand, and then stood rigid, tiny hands at its sides, as if unable to move. Morgan bent her face down to it, and the little figure crouched down on her hand, the picture of terror. Its colour changed, like paint that fades in the sun – no longer blue and green like the bluebells, but a washed-out yellow; and it shook with tiny sobs. The other sprites cleared back in a ring and stood trembling, those at the front also losing their colour. Above the trees a cloud passed over the sun.

'Oh, Morgan!' Vivian cried. 'Why did you have to spoil it? It was all so lovely—'

'Pooh, stupid things,' said Morgan, and shook the fairy off her hand, like a fly. It fell, though lightly, and they saw it scramble to the others and the whole crowd, now faded and hardly visible, slipped back among the flowers and was gone.

'Silly things,' said Morgan, wiping her hands together as if to rid them of some dirt. 'I'll show you some that are much more fun.'

She led the way back towards the farmstead, a cluster of thatched huts connected by covered passageways, and went round the buildings to where the cattle-byres and slaughterhouse were. Here was a stony slope, evil-smelling and full of flies, where the blood from the slaughterhouse drained down into the lower ground.

'We're not allowed here,' said Vivian.

'I can go where I like,' was Morgan's retort. 'Look down there.'

Where they looked the blood lay thick, and over it was a clustering crowd of little beings, human in shape, black and harsh-red like hornets, with some touches of yellow. They were as small and light as the woodland fairies, but different. They were crowding over the pools of blood, sucking it up like the flies, and squirming and writhing together. A few seemed to be embracing, but most were fighting.

Morgan watched the scene, chuckling with pleasure. 'Go it, you little bastards,' she exclaimed.

'Oh Morgan, you mustn't say things like that,' Vivian protested faintly.

'I'll say what I like. They *are* little bastards.' She took one of them up on her hand, as she had with the fairy. The creature had a thin tail like a mouse's, and there seemed to be a sharp point at the end of it, like a sting. Struggling, the little imp plunged its sting again and again into Morgan's wrist, but she did not seem to feel anything.

Morgause looked on in fascination. 'Oh, Morgan, it's dangerous – oh, you are brave – oh, take care; doesn't it hurt you?'

'Not a bit,' laughed Morgan, as the little thing brought its head down and bit her with tiny, sharp teeth. 'Here, you try it,' and she turned, not to Morgause, but to Vivian, and held out the little imp to her. Vivian screamed and ran, and Morgan ran after her, shrieking with derision, holding the devilkin between finger and thumb as if to thrust it upon her. Vivian fled in terror, thinking any minute she would feel the little horror planted on her back. She ran, with Morgan in pursuit, and at last saw the door of the small wattle church that belonged to the farm. She ran in and pulled the leather curtain to, across the doorway. Morgan stopped, and then walked past slowly. It was quiet in the little church, dark but for the lamp that burned before the altar. Vivian felt safe here. When she emerged, after some minutes, the other two were ahead of her walking home. Vivian followed quietly at a distance.

3. Greater Witches

The next year they came again to Roseland, and the next. That year, when they were ten, there was a surprise for them at the farm. On the eve of St John's Day, Dame Olwen visited them. She was smiling and genial, as if she brought good news. This was unusual, for she was usually a dour and reserved woman. She had long passed from the position of Head Nurse to that of Governess, though she still kept her title of La Nourrice.

'I am taking you all on a visit,' she said, 'to see some friends of mine. Important people. You must get ready.'

She called for tubs of hot water and, to their surprise, she made them wash themselves all over. Then she washed the hair of each one, brushed and combed it out all its length – the blonde, the red and the jet black. Then she bid them put on clean linen smocks, but to their wonder she did not make them wear their best dresses, only such as they would wear to go riding in the woods. Nor did she make them put on any jewellery, except for necklaces of large beads: blue enamel for Morgause, cornelian for Vivian, jet for Morgan. They wondered, but asked no questions. Olwen La Nourrice was not one who answered questions readily.

In late midsummer twilight they set out on their ponies. Olwen led them right into the woods that surrounded the farm, on into the deepest and most deserted part. The sun went down behind the thick green and a translucent blue darkness closed round them. All was tranquil and hushed, but the wood was softly, sweetly alive. Then, far off, they heard the sound of pipes and tabors. Olwen halted and dismounted, directing the girls to do the same. She tied the horses to a tree and led the way now on foot, deep along a narrow, twisting pathway. Presently they saw, through the trees, the leaping light of a fire. As they drew nearer they saw that the light came from a large bonfire in the centre of a dell. It formed a pool, a globe of light in the darkness of the woods, glowing back from the green foliage and the brown-red trunks. There seemed to be hundreds of people, moving, passing, circling around the fire, but the silhouettes of the nearest prevented the girls from glimpsing any details of those on the far side of the fire. Before they had a chance to see more, Olwen hurried them away down a side path. There they found a rough arrangement of freshly cut branches on which many people's garments were laid out. A grey-faced girl, who seemed to be a simpleton, was taking care of them.

'Now,' said Olwen, briskly, 'take off your clothes. Yes, all of them.' And seeing their startled faces, 'Yes. This is what you must do. I as well. You will find that all the company are the same.'

Very coolly she proceeded to undress. As she turned aside to step out of her clothes, the three girls drew together into an excited huddle. Slowly, they followed her example.

'It's the witches,' Vivian whispered.

'Oooh – it's the witches!' Morgause suppressed an excited squeal.

'I know,' said Morgan.

Olwen stood before them now, naked, her head held high, not at all the servant she was in Tintagel. She beckoned to the three girls to follow her. They stepped into the firelight, ivory-white, slender, graceful little striplings, their small breasts hardly distinguishing them from boys, their hair – the blonde, the red, the black – falling down their backs.

The circle round the fire was not as numerous as had at first seemed – thirty or forty, all women, all naked. As with their faces, so their naked bodies were of all sorts, handsome and ugly, young and old. But distinctions of high and low, rich and poor, were all lost. There was nothing to distinguish the noble lady from the tinker's wife. Nothing but their own persons. All wore their hair flowing free, golden locks or scanty, grey wisps. Each wore around her neck a collar of large round beads, the sign of the Great Mother.

All seemed the same to the girls' bewildered eyes; but across the fire was one with authority, tall and well-shaped; her dark hair, unlike the others', was piled high on her head and crowned with a headdress of silver horns. The upper part of her face was hidden by a black mask, all but the brilliant eyes that stared out through the eyeholes.

Olwen led the girls round the fire, going from left to

right, round the curve, and to the left, against the way of the sun. Morgause was first behind Olwen, then Vivian, then Morgan, all in line, but holding hands fore and aft. Olwen halted before the masked woman and made a deep obeisance. The masked woman greeted her; her voice was deep and powerful, but certainly that of a lady.

'Hail, Olwen, trusty companion. So you have brought the three. Let me see them.'

Olwen led Morgause forward first. The masked woman extended her hand to her, which Morgause took and, as she had been taught, curtseyed, but how awkward it was with no clothes! The masked woman raised her, looked earnestly into her face with those gleaming eyes through the mask, and passed her hand round Morgause's face, caressing the curve of her chin.

'She'll do,' she said to Olwen. 'This one will make a witch, though she'll always follow where others lead. Bring her to me in seven years' time.'

Then Olwen led Vivian up. Vivian felt the lady's hand cold as ice, and a tremor ran through her. She wished she had some clothes on, any clothes. The masked lady smiled, and caressed her face as she had Morgause's.

'This one – perhaps. She will go her own way. In seven years' time we shall see.'

Vivian felt glad when the lady released her hand and she could step back. Now Olwen brought forward Morgan.

The masked lady gave a little cry of astonishment and threw up her hands. Then she sank to the ground on her knees before Morgan.

'It is she. Lady, I recognize you – you have come back

to us, as foretold, after ages of ages. You are she. Be gracious to me and confirm me in my office till your time has come.'

Without any prompting Morgan answered, 'I do,' and laid her hand on the head of the masked lady, who then rose to her feet and addressed the circle, her voice trembling.

'Hear all of you and behold, for this is Morgan, and here I name her Le Fay, for that is who she is.'

And at that the whole assembly sighed deeply, as if they were profoundly moved. Vivian could feel a kind of shiver running round the circle. But Morgan herself stood unmoved, with a small, gentle, unperturbed smile on her deep, red lips. She stood steadily by the side of the witch-queen, while all the witches filed past her and each one kissed her cheek. It seemed to Vivian to take a very long time, and Morgause's attention was wandering to the space behind the circle where food was laid out on a long table.

When the circle had been all round the fire and each returned to her own place, the witch-queen addressed the three girls again.

'Now, our new little witches, we are allowed to grant each of you a wish. Name your wish and we'll grant it to you, if in our power. You, Morgan Le Fay?'

'I have no need of wishes,' said Morgan.

'True, and wisely answered. Now you, Vivian?'

'I should like,' said Vivian hesitantly, 'to have knowledge – to know things – to be wise – so that I could do good to people, heal their sicknesses, turn bad luck to good, make them happy—' She stopped, aware of the silence around her. The witch-queen spoke.

'Knowledge you shall certainly have, but wisdom – which do you want: wisdom or knowledge?'

'But are they not the same?' she asked, greatly daring.

'No, my child, they are not the same, but you are over-young yet to know that. You have much to learn. Also you wish to do good, but you have much to learn also about what you have been taught to call good and evil. You may yet have to learn that they are much more alike than are knowledge and wisdom . . .' She gave a strange smile, and Vivian could feel the eyes focusing on her from behind the mask. 'But go your ways, child. Knowledge you shall have, and wisdom you may yet attain, but not, I think, from us.' She turned from her. 'And now, my fair-haired Morgause, what is your wish?'

And Morgause spoke clearly and without hesitation: 'I want a baby brother.'

A shrill burst of laughter went round the circle of glistening bodies, and then a nodding of heads together and a chattering as of gossips and heads turned with covert smiles. The witch-queen looked down at her, and the smile below the line of the black mask broadened.

'Why, that's for your mother to wish, but I believe it might come to you yet, and bring you more than you ever supposed – and to more than you. But you will have to wait. Go in peace now.'

She waved her hand in dismissal and Olwen led them back from the circle. The pipes and tabors started again and the women prepared to dance.

'Come now,' said Olwen, 'we must get dressed and go home.'

'Oh, can't we stop a little?' said Morgause. 'They're just going to dance – and the feast . . .'

'Fair enough, greedy-guts,' laughed Olwen. 'Get your clothes on and I'll get you your share of the cakes. But you can't see the dancing till you're a great deal older.'

Seeing them hastily into their clothes, Olwen, now clothed also, led them away behind the circle to the cooking fires, where even Morgause's appetite was satisfied. But Olwen would not let them go back into the circle, though the infectious rhythms called to them. She led them away, still chewing on pork bones, through the wood to their horses and back to the farmstead.

As they stood in the moonlight on the threshold of the hut where they lodged, Morgause asked, 'Nurse Olwen, when shall we become real witches?'

Olwen was a shadow against the dark blue sky as she stood over them. 'Not for a long while yet. You must be old enough, perhaps seventeen. But you can be preparing.'

'Oh, how, how do we prepare?'

'Learn as much as you can. Your father will soon be providing a tutor for you.'

'Oh,' said Morgause, petulant at the thought of learning.

'And you must renounce your Christian baptism.'

'That's all right,' said Morgause. 'I don't care. What about you, Vivian?'

'I don't know,' said Vivian slowly. 'I'm not so sure that I want to do that. What about Morgan?'

'Morgan was never baptized,' said Olwen.

4. Wizard Schoolmaster

They had many more summers at Roseland, but they did not see the witches again for some years. When they were turned twelve and back at Tintagel for the autumn, one bright frosty morning, their father brought a visitor into their big four-square chamber in the tower.

'I've brought you a tutor, daughters,' he said. 'He'll teach you everything you ought to know. And you'll obey him as you would obey me, or he has my leave to beat you.'

Gorlais beckoned towards the darker recesses of the chamber. 'Here he is. You shall know him as Merlin.'

He came out of the shadows. He was dressed in a green linen robe like a priest's cassock. A square of green linen was laid smoothly over his head and fell down behind his ears. He had the appearance of between thirty-five and forty, but there was a depth in his brilliant blue eyes of dark cornflower, that made him seem ageless. He was broad in the shoulder and strong, but not unduly tall. He had a wide forehead, beautifully proportioned to his straight nose, powerful chin, and trim short black beard.

Jet-black hair, like Morgan's, flowed from under the green headcloth, above expressive eyebrows that ran up into little horn-like points at their top. He looked the girls up and down with a critical eye, then he looked at Olwen, who sketched a half curtsey and withdrew without a word.

'I'll leave you with them,' said the Duke. 'Let me know if you have any trouble.'

'It will not be necessary,' he said as the Duke left them.

Merlin courteously saw him to the door and then turned back to the girls. He had noted them as one blonde, one brunette and one redhead, but as he looked at them now they were all three identical redheads, and dancing round him. He turned to follow their motion, and they were all blondes, now all black-haired, now two redheads and one blonde, now six of them, of all colours, spinning round and round him, giggling and cackling. A hand swept out from their circle and pulled his head-veil away. Other hands seized his shoulders and spun him.

Only for a moment did this last until Merlin regained his composure. Then he stamped his foot on the ground, once, twice, thrice. There was stillness and silence. The girls felt as if a tingling shock had come up from the earth and struck them instantly rigid. They stood like statues, only their rapid breathing breaking the silence.

'All right,' said Morgan. 'We give in. We know you're clever.'

'You'd better, you baggage,' came the reply. The tension relaxed and the gripping spell left them.

'Is that the way you speak to the Duke's daughter?' said Morgause, pouting and dimpling at him.

'Yes, it is. You're Morgause, and I know all about you from your father. And you're Vivian, and I know all about you too. But you, Morgan . . .'

They stood confronting each other stiffly. Her hand reached out to his breast-pendant, but she lifted her face and looked him in the eyes, and he looked fixedly down on her. So they remained a long minute.

'Oh yes, we have met before,' he said softly and with a distant smile. 'You are more newly into this world than am I, this time, but I can recognize you and you can recognize me. Just for an instant, look and remember while the portal stands open. In a moment it will close again.'

Briefly Morgan's eyes gazed forward unfocused and a smile turned the corners of her mouth. 'Oh, I know you,' she said with a voice that belied her years. And then the moment passed and they turned from each other, laughing. Vivian was aware that something had passed between them and deep down, for the first time, she felt a twinge of envy.

Merlin picked up a bundle of books from a corner trestle and dropped them on the table.

'Now,' he said, with stern authority, 'this is your school-room where we will work together every day from Nones to noon.'

They dared not gainsay him now.

'What will you teach us?' asked Vivian, curious about the nature of the man. 'Are you going to teach us magic?'

They settled into the chairs around a table. Merlin

smiled, perhaps a little sourly. 'Magic? Why, it seems you know some already.'

Vivian and Morgause blushed; not so Morgan.

'Oh that's nothing,' Morgan said. 'We want to learn *real* magic. *You* know.'

'Yes, I know,' Merlin replied. 'Well, perhaps I will teach you magic when you are ready, if you are able to learn it. But you must learn a great deal first.'

'What must we learn?' Vivian asked.

'Why, first to read and write. You will get nowhere without that.'

'I've tried it and I don't like it,' said Morgause.

'Nevertheless, you must learn it first of all, or I can teach you nothing else. Then you must learn Latin, Greek and Hebrew, without which you cannot understand the great books.'

'I'll learn them if I please to,' said Morgan defiantly. 'And after Latin, Greek and Hebrew, what next?'

'Why, the *trivium* and the *quadrivium*.'

'And what in mercy's name are those?' said Morgause. She had found some nuts in her pocket and was chewing them.

'The Three and the Four: Grammar, Logic and Rhetoric, and then Arithmetic, Geometry, Music and Astronomy.'

'Oh God's grief!' cried Morgause, shrugging her plump shoulders. 'I'll never manage all that.'

'There's only one thing that sounds nice,' said Morgan, 'and that's Music. We'd like to learn Music. Do you know any magic songs?'

'I do,' he said, and now he smiled a little.

'We know a magic song – the song of He and She. Do you know it?'

'I certainly do,' he said. 'It is the one that begins:

Oh, she looked out of the window,
As white as any milk,
And he looked into the window,
As black as any silk—'

'Yes, that's the one,' Vivian broke in eagerly.

'Only it's ever so old,' interrupted Morgause. 'It's all wrong, I'm sure. Why is it "as black as any silk"? Silk isn't black, or at least not always.'

'It is when it's a magician's conjuring robe – always black silk.' Merlin smiled, for he felt they were establishing contact now.

'But you're not in black silk,' objected Morgause. 'You're just in green linen. Are you a magician or aren't you?'

'I'm an Ovate,' he explained. 'The Ovates learn and teach. Next year I shall be a full Druid, and then I shall wear white. But there are times for wearing the black silk conjuring robe. Now, where did you learn that song?'

The girls looked from one to the other.

'Indeed, we don't know,' said Vivian. 'It might have been from Olwen. Oh, I don't know. Seems we've always known it.'

'Let's sing it now,' said Morgan. 'Sing it and dance it in the proper way.'

They moved the table back and left a clear space in the centre of the room. Morgan stood in the middle with Merlin by her – it was assumed that she would be 'She' to his 'He', and the other two the chorus. Morgause and Vivian circled them as if they were making a ring, and began.

Oh, she looked out of the window,
As white as any milk,
And he looked into the window,
As black as any silk.
Hullo, hullo, hullo, hullo,
you coal-black, pitch-black Smith,
Oh what is, pray, your silly song?
You ne'er shall change my maiden name,
that I have kept so long.
I'd rather die a maid, she said,
and lie dead in my grave,
Than I'd have such a nasty, musty, rusty, fusty
Coal-Black Smith—
A Maiden I will die!

The two in the middle mimed the action, the other two making the frame of the window from where 'She' looked out and 'He' looked in. In the next verse 'She' escaped into the circle and ran from him, and 'He' pursued her, both acting out the bird and beast.

Then she became a duck, a duck,
a duck all on the stream,
And he became a water-dog,
and fetched her back again.
Hullo, hullo, hullo, hullo,
you coal-black, pitch-black Smith.

At the end of the verse Merlin caught Morgan and kissed her, as the game always demanded. At the touch something electrical seemed to hit him – not just the sensuous attraction of her childhood beauty, the sweetness, the freshness – nor the involuntary response, hard to repress, aroused in him by her unripe sexuality. But something stranger and even more dangerous. She suffered the kiss, absently, and then drew back from him.

'Oh, but we're doing it all wrong,' she said. '*She* should be chasing, and *He* running away. You see, we've never played this with a man before, but now I'm sure that's how it should be. Look, we'll go on, but we'll do it as I say.'

And so they started the next verse, as Morgan amended it.

Then he became a hare, a hare,
a hare all on the green,
And she became a greyhound-dog,
and fetched him back again.
Hullo, hullo, hullo, hullo,
you coal-black, pitch-black Smith.

Now she was pursuing and he was running before her. To Vivian's mind the scene formed itself clear and visible – the rolling green down, Merlin the hare, his dancing eyebrows above his bright eyes, like the hare's erected ears, as he dodged and turned over the grassy hillocks and sometimes halted and sat up to look back and mock his pursuer. But there was Morgan, fleet and slender, stretched out on all four slim legs at full length, gaining on him. Then snap! She had the hare by his long ears, and carried him kicking back. She was laughing and claiming another kiss from him. This time she seemed to want it.

Now the final verse began:

Then he became a fly, a fly,
a fly all in the air,
And she became a spider black,

and fetched him to her lair.
Hullo, hullo, hullo, hullo . . .

Vivian saw it even more plainly. Up high in clear space Merlin hovered as a fly. What kind? Surely not one of the dirty black houseflies, nor even the dirtier bluebottles, but something transparent, slender and grey, like one of those crane flies. But above him loomed Morgan in the centre of her web, her eight curling legs black and yellow, her eyes many-faceted and glistening; and already she had Merlin in her clutches, swaddled round with gossamer. She handled the inert figure like one accustomed to the work. And now she brought her great pincer-like mandibles down over his head – one grip and it would all be up for the fly.

Vivian broke into the game, shrieking, 'No, no, Morgan! Don't, Morgan!'

She caught at something – the spider, or Morgan's arm, she could not tell – but the spell was broken. The song tailed away before its last line. Merlin, gently freeing himself from Morgan, sat down panting. His face was very white.

'Thanks, Vivian,' he said. 'The pace was a little too hot for me. I must remember, I'm an old man now, and mustn't do these things.'

'You're not an old man,' cried Vivian. He beamed on her and a little colour came back into his cheeks. Vivian placed herself in front of him and turned to face Morgan.

'Morgan, you're not to hurt him. I won't let you do anything to him, so there!'

'Oh, silly,' said Morgan, 'it's only a game. I wasn't going to hurt him. Nothing but a game, you goose.'

'Maybe – but I don't like it all the same.'

Merlin drew the little girl towards his knees. 'Thank you, my little champion, but, you know, I think I can take care of myself.'

'You may think so,' said Vivian frowning, 'but you don't know the horrid things she can do.'

'Don't I?' he said, smiling. 'I think I do, though.' He looked Morgan over, critically, while she reflected his looks back with her bold black eyes. He shook his head as if to break free from such shadowy thoughts. 'But never mind that. Let's all mind our own business, shall we? And our business now is to learn. But what about you?' He turned to Morgause, feeling perhaps that he had not given enough attention to the third sister.

Morgause was munching an apple and waited till she had the last bite in her mouth before replying. 'Well, what about me, then?'

'Do you want to learn magic too?'

'I want you to do some magic for me. You're a magic man, aren't you?'

'Well, if I were . . . Why, what do you want, then?'

'I want a baby brother,' she said. 'I want you to make a magic so our mother will give me a baby brother.'

He started violently. 'By the gods, child, what—' and then, quickly recovering his poise, 'My dear, that's for your mother to say, and of course, your father, too. That's not a thing I can do.'

'Yes you can,' she persisted. 'You're magic; you can do everything.'

'Oh I daresay, I daresay. But not that. Now, not another word. Time we began lessons. Here's your horn-books, and your slates, and your slate pencils.'

And they settled down quietly to work after a time, and the schoolroom grew silent. He waited for them to finish writing out the capital letters from the hornbook, and rested his eyes on a bright point of light, where the sun struck the edge of a silver cup – a bright point of light . . .

He came to his senses with a start.

'A baby brother, indeed,' he said to himself. 'I don't know, little Morgause. It might be, it might be. We are all instruments of Destiny. Wait and see, you little witches, wait and see.'

5. Knight Errant

Britain was a lawless place in those days. Since the Romans had left there was no real rule or authority, nor much contact between one region and another. Small communities, cut off by unrepaired roads and dangerous wildernesses, drew in upon themselves, knowing little of the world outside, or even of their neighbours. Small landowners set themselves up as petty lords, and dispensed justice or injustice as suited them. For one good ruler there were a dozen bad ones. Might was right; tyranny and cruelty abounded. In many places fierce foreigners in long black ships came raiding. These were often no better than the tyrants they replaced. The men of peace, the monks and priests of the Old Church, died martyrs or fled from the burning churches into the western mountains.

And here and there in all this confusion, it was not to be wondered at if things still more evil survived. In the darkest impenetrable woods, in the clefts of the mountains, in the honeycomb caves underground, strange creatures still lurked, survivors from earlier times. Great worms, bat-winged birds, some, it might be said, not altogether of this world, half-in and half-out of the Shadowland. Hauntings and baleful influences. Such things always thrive on thoughts of hatred. Time had been when the Christian priests of the Celtic Church, saying their masses daily in the white decorated villas, had kept these things at bay. Even before them, the white-clad Druids had warded them off with their good magic. But now it was said that some of the barons protected and even nourished the monsters, and who dared say what they nourished them *on*?

But there were still, in one place and another, people who remembered better things. One such family was that of Bors, and his brothers Ector, Torion and Lioncel, who lived on the edge of the great Forest of Anderida. Their father, Briareus, and their mother Elena, remembered better times, and their grandfather Constans remembered the Romans. In their moated grange, a farmhouse solidly built of wood surrounded by a deep moat, and able to withstand a siege if necessary, they did their best to keep alive the old civilized ways. They had their priest, who said Mass daily in their little chapel, for the family and a few friends – Brian, Ulphius, Brastias – some of them with their wives, and all young. Meeting often, they would wish with all their hearts for better things, and talked of banding together to root out injustices. Sometimes they would take action together to right some of the worst wrongs, but their power was little, and whether there were others in other places who were like-minded, they had no means of knowing.

Two legacies they had from Roman days, beside their house: a few pieces of fine Roman armour, in particular the towering helmets and the breast-plates; and a breeding strain of tall black horses, taller by many hands than the stocky British ponies. It was said that the ancestors of those horses came from Rome, long ago. Certainly they were not like any other horses ever seen in these parts or, as far as was known, in Britain. A man on one of those horses could command respect.

So sometimes, mounted on those same black horses, these young men would ride out, in twos and threes, or sometimes alone, in search of wrongs to right, a monster to exterminate or a victim to rescue. It was thus that Torion, the youngest brother of the four, had ridden out one day alone, in search of adventure. Setting out from the borders of Anderida on his tall black horse, he had ridden south and west. He had heard of a strange wild region in the extreme west where the land stretched out into the sea, and then was no more – Land's End.

Late one afternoon he came to a place he had heard spoken of as Dozmary Pool. *Douce-Maree* – Sweet Lake. But all that was sweet about it, he found, was that it was not salty. It was a desolate, weedy, slimy pool, desolate and sinister, alone atop the barren moors, with a river neither feeding it nor draining it. The place felt bad. Despite the blueness of the sky and the warmth of the sun, the spot was cold and unwelcoming, as if abandoned by nature. A wind hugged the ground and rustled through the grasses beside the lake and across the moors. Torion shivered. Something was wrong here.

Searching carefully he found it. A nasty thing of the lizard kind. Not very large, but dangerous, lurking in a dim crevice in the most stagnant corner of the lake. The bones that surrounded its lair showed how dangerous it was. There were human bones among them. As Torion approached the beast hissed and reared its long neck up from the cave. Torion dealt with it effectively, as he had done with others. The beast may have frightened merchants and farmers and unwary travellers, but it was no match for a knight. Torion's horse was as used to such encounters as he was, and knew how to react. True, it was no easy fight. The worm was sinuous and slippery, twisting this way and that as it tried to spit its venom at its opponent. But Torion had the advantage and with his sword split open the beast's skull and then cut off its head. The ichor oozed green into the lake where it hissed, bubbled, and was silent.

Torion left the obscene carcass, with the scavenging birds already gathering, and rode away with a sense of mission accomplished. He was tired now and would have welcomed an inn, but there was none in sight over the bare, treeless landscape. He pressed on as the sun began to sink.

The rough track he was following began to dip downhill and, just as the sun's rim sank below the horizon ahead of him, he saw a light in a hollow below. It seemed to be coming from within a wood. All day he had seen no trees, and this was reassuring – there would be people there, woodcutters, perhaps a village. He pressed on.

Descending the hill he lost sight of the light and the woods closed in upon him. Then he began to hear music, very faint and far off, at first more rhythm than tune, just the deep pulsations of drums and tabors, and possibly of feet; then the melody of country pipes was added. Music! Who was dancing in the woods at sunset? Well, there were country revels, shepherds' dances, huntsmen's celebrations – it need be nothing stranger. But could it –

his heart beat a little faster – could it perhaps be the Little People? He had heard of them in fireside tales, which told that they were still to be seen in certain places, a weird and beautiful sight, but dangerous. What an adventure if it were . . . He spurred his horse forward.

At last he found the elusive gleam of light, red and flashing – the light of a bonfire. A gap through the trees on a slight rise showed him the picture at a distance. People, women with their long hair unbound, dancing in a ring around a fire. They were still too far away to see clearly. Oh yes, surely it must be the Little People – yet not so little. He closed in on them. A path round a screen of thick bushes suddenly brought him close to them, and he almost cried out in amazement. They were all stark naked.

Beyond all doubt he had fallen among witches.

There was nothing alluring about their nakedness. Young and old they were, some comely and some hideous, all sorts and kinds, their unbound hair golden or black or grey. The ruddy light of the fire played upon their skins, the shadows accentuating their curves. He was suddenly surrounded by them. They did not touch him, but they glared menacingly at him, their hands like claws, their teeth bared. The music had ceased abruptly and he heard only a low growling noise, like threatening cats. His horse stood still, shivering and running with sweat, its ears laid back. He could do nothing.

A voice spoke over the heads of the crowded women.

'What shall we do with him?'

'Tear him to pieces,' several voices chorused.

'Too quick and easy!' said another.

'Shall we,' said the first voice, 'do as Diana did to

Acteon? Shall we let his horse be his executioner?' The voice paused, then went on, 'No, not the horse. Why should we destroy the dumb brute? We've no quarrel with the beasts, only with men. This we will do. We will loose the Barghest upon him from behind. It has fasted long and is hungry.'

'Yes, yes, the Barghest,' came a chorus of cries. 'The Barghest! The Barghest!'

They drew back from him, still not touching him. He could not understand it, for they seemed to be letting him go. One of them turned his horse's head with a jerk to the bridle, and motioned him to go on.

'Go!' some of them shouted. 'Go in peace. The kind of peace we'll give you. Go, and the Barghest attend you—'

He urged his horse into a canter until he was well away from the witches. The thought of them made him feel slightly sick. What was it they said? *The Barghest*. What was that? Dimly he recalled fireside tales about the bear-ghost or the ghost-bear. It was not a bear, though – they mostly spoke of a dog, a black dog, on certain lonely roads. He recalled stories of packmen and pedlars frightened by it – but as roads grew worse and men travelled less, the bogies outside were forgotten. There were enough horrors in the depths of their own houses. Outside were *They*, and nobody liked to speculate much on what *They* were, or give them names to bring them closer. He remembered an old house he had once visited, a ruined Roman villa, where the owner had worked a pattern of little stones into the stone pavement. It had shown a large black dog and the word *CAVE – Beware*.

As he slackened his horse's pace to a walk along the dark pathway he heard footsteps behind him. *Pad, pad,*

pad – soft, quick and deliberate, following him. He turned awkwardly in his cumbersome armour and, where a faint gleam of the rising moon illumined the road, he saw it and laughed aloud with relief. A small black dog, no more than a spaniel, was trotting along. Well, was this all their Barghest amounted to? It was a nasty little dog, though. It yapped at him and showed sharp little teeth and hostile eyes. Torion took up a bunch of twigs that hung by his saddle to brush away flies and brandished it at the dog, shouting at it to go away. The dog turned and pattered out of sight. So, that was that. He laughed again and went on his way.

It must have been after midnight; he was tired and anxious to find shelter. He was accustomed to camping out if needful, but this dark wood that seemed to go on and on offered no good camping place. He would have to press on in hope, weary as he was. Then he heard the footsteps again. Oh, curse that silly little dog. He turned to wave it away again, and there it was, but bigger this time. A great hound, like a farmer's lurcher, as black as before, and with the same menacing eyes and teeth. This would heed no fly-whisk. He drew his sword and waved it at the beast which, surprisingly, silently turned and sloped away. How strange, and rather disquieting, Torion mused, but, better move on. Perhaps he had disposed of it this time.

No. After a mile the *pad, pad, pad* returned, heavier and more lumbering than before. He could feel his horse starting to tremble. This time, looking back, the thing that was following was bigger than any hound he had ever seen. It was as big as a horse – long-legged, straight-backed, heavy-jowled, with a tail that curved away like a bow. It was as black as night, with great luminous eyes that gazed down on him.

Wildly, Torion waved his sword. Without any sign of fear the beast turned, flourishing its long tail, and retreated back down the road. Torion went on uneasily, still moving steadily – not to canter, not to gallop. If he did, would that beast come thundering after him?

Again he heard the padding of the footsteps. He turned. There it was, bigger than ever. But it was no longer a dog, but a bear, huge and shaggy, on its hind legs, taller than a man, almost blacking out the full moon. His ire rising, Torion thrust towards it with his sword raised. And again the thing turned and vanished into the woods. Torion sat there in the saddle, puzzled. He was sweating cold and panting. His horse pulled against the rein and would have bolted.

Suddenly, at the side of the road, appeared a woman. She was wrapped and veiled in soft floating grey, and all that Torion could see of her was that she seemed young and slender, and her hair was dark red. She stepped closer and spoke in an urgent whisper, as if something might overhear them.

'You must turn and fight it,' she said. 'If you go on walking away it gets bigger every time. It will be bigger next time, and the time after that, bigger than you can ever imagine. Fight it now. I will help you. Give me your sword.'

'Give you my sword? Never!'

'You must if I am to help you. Be quick!'

'But you're one of the witches.'

'I am not a witch, though I was amongst them. Quick, give me your sword, for God's sake.'

'My sword is consecrated, and I may not.'

'I tell you, give me your sword in the Name of the Father, and of the Son, and of the Holy Ghost.'

'And how shall I fight if I do?'

'Take your spear. I will hold your sword behind you as a cross. It is the only way.'

He turned his sword, which he was still holding, and gave it to her by the hilt. She took it and turned it crosswise, holding it by the blade. He set his spear in its rest as to charge, and wheeled about as he heard the footsteps again.

The thing that advanced on him was terrifying. Larger than a bear – larger than any beast he had ever seen or heard of – black and shaggy, tusked like a boar, fiery-eyed, with luminous foam dripping from its open jaws. It advanced upright, menacing with its uplifted paws.

'Now charge!' the woman cried, holding the cruciform sword steady. He gave the spur and the familiar toss to the reins, as if in the tourney, and the good horse carried him forward, right towards that mass of fur and flesh. The beast hurried its advance and the two forces met. The long spear found its mark. Torion heard the beast shriek and felt the drag of its weight on the spear, but the impetus of its own charge carried it onwards, struggling, along the length of the spear, as a wounded boar will do. But a boar-spear has a long bar across it to deal with just such a struggle. Torion's spear had not. On and on the beast struggled, the claws thrashing in front. The horse, plunging in terror, was within range, but its armour saved its eyes and breast. Torion was dimly conscious that the woman behind him was holding the sword from which light streamed and, as it shone, the monster's struggles weakened, and finally ceased. It fell, dragging the spear to the ground out of Torion's grasp.

'Quick now,' the woman urged, handing him the sword. 'Cut off its head.'

Dismounting, he did so, and stood back amazed as the great beast began to dissolve away, like a pool of water drying under the sun. It became a small shrinking black puddle, and then nothing. The woman stepped forward and put her foot, brown, bare and firm, on the spot where the last vestige had vanished. And the first faint light of daybreak began to creep through the woods.

Torion looked down at the woman and really saw her for the first time. She was the most beautiful girl he had ever seen. Her dark red hair was lighter and more glowing as the daylight visited it. Her eyes were what struck him the most – so large and deep-set and haunting, a strange bluish-green, like turquoise, or like the sky seen through beech-leaves in spring. Her mouth was like a wild rose, and her face, pale and softly flushed, was also like a rose, its shape and form something more than merely perfect. She stood by his horse's head, caressing it with long white hands, soothing away its fear.

Torion tried to speak, but found his voice was caught by emotion.

'Lady—'

'Yes?' She looked up at him smiling.

'My lady, I must thank you from the bottom of my soul. But who are you? What is your name?'

'I am Vivian. I am one of three sisters and we live in the castle of Tintagel.'

Torion could still not bring himself to speak. Vivian

encouraged him. 'Well? What would you ask me? What can I do for you?'

'Oh lady,' he said, completely lost, 'oh, fairest lady – I love you, I adore you, I worship you—'

'That is sweet of you,' she said with a disarming smile. 'Say no more. I think you are not quite yourself yet. You must be very weary, are you not?'

'Oh, not too weary to know that you are – you are—'

'Come now,' she said, 'no more talk. I will take you where you can find rest and refreshment. Let me sit behind you and I will guide you to where you should go.'

Her brisk tone made him pull himself together. Unaided she sprang to the crupper behind him and piloted him through forest paths. To feel her slender, firm body pressed to his back was almost more than he could bear. She leaned over his shoulder and whispered directions to him.

'You must attend to me,' she said sternly, 'or I'll slap your face. Stop being a silly boy, or we'll never get there.'

They reached the boundary of the forest, beyond which was bare downland and the sea; and at the forest's edge was a peasant's hut. Vivian slipped quickly to the ground and knocked on the door. An elderly woman answered.

'My lady, you're here early.'

'Bless you, Mother Woodedge. I know I can always count on you. This knight needs food and a bed, and stabling for his horse. Both horse and man have fought a battle. Will you see to him?'

'Why, willingly, my lady. Come in, Sir Knight, and welcome. Be you wounded? No; thank the Powers. Come your ways, sir.'

In the hut Torion shed his armour. In the yard he was given a bowl of water where he washed. Then, settled down, they shared frumenty with cream and honey. Only then did Vivian speak again.

'Now, tell me your name.'

'I am Torion, the son of Briareus. We live on the other side of Anderida Forest. I and my brothers and some friends are vowed to ride as far as we may range to rid the land of monstrous beasts and tyrannous men.'

'You've made a good riddance of one such this night,' she said.

'With your help. But the land is full of them. We can do only so much.'

'I know. Our tutor Merlin has told us many times.'

'Merlin?' he said, looking sharply up. 'I have heard that name. Your tutor? Whence comes he?'

'Why, I don't know. He's just our tutor.'

'I should like to meet him. We have heard – our father has told us – that there are other men like us in the land, who would like to see better things and better ways, if only we had a leader. Perhaps such a man will come some day—'

'Perhaps he will,' Vivian mused. 'You must have faith, and be ready.'

'We shall. But, lady, may I not see you again, perhaps to talk of Merlin?'

'I think not,' she said. 'Not for the present. I must go home, and you must sleep and restore your strength.'

'Oh, how can I sleep for thinking of you?'

'Look,' she said, pointing one finger at him. 'For this time only, as you think of me you will sleep, deeply and sweetly. Now, good rest to you.' She rose quickly from the bench and hurried from the hut. He was already overcome with drowsiness. The old lady led him away to a soft pallet of dried ferns, and he was asleep while still in her hands.

Vivian took her way home to the farm, walking thoughtfully in the fresh morning. Such a charming young man, and one of the right kind, such as Merlin was seeking. But not a lover for her. No, there was only one man in the world for her now, and that was Merlin.

6. Belle Dame Sans Merci

The homestead where the three girls spent their summers had grown, in those five years or so, into a comfortable farmhouse. The girls had a pleasant bower, or upper room, with a window with shutters, and outside they had made a little enclosed garden. Into this garden in the fresh morning Vivian came walking, a little dazed for lack of sleep, and found her sisters, also rather sleepy, but at least having had a few hours in bed.

'Well, Vivian dear,' said Morgause, with a yawn. 'You left us after the dancing. I hope you found a nice partner to walk home with. Took you all night, did it?'

'Oh, she found a partner, right enough,' said Morgan, '*and* spent all night with him. And yet she wasted her time. She didn't sleep with him.'

'She doesn't have to *sleep,*' said Morgause, giggling.

'No, I didn't sleep with him,' said Vivian, red-faced.

'I know you didn't,' said Morgan. 'More fool you.'

Vivian rounded on Morgan. 'How do you know?'

'How? You ought to know. You have the Clear-Sight like the rest of us. I was with you and saw everything.'

Vivian's face was alight with anger.

'You saw? You followed me with the Sight? How dare you! I never have any privacy! Am I never free of you?'

'My dear,' said Morgan in her most condescending voice, 'you must improve your art. If you don't know how to safeguard your mind against me, why, I can't help it.'

Vivian was speechless with mortification, and turned away. Morgan pursued her.

'That's a lovely man of yours, and you wasted your opportunity like a fool. Couldn't you take the good fortune that came your way? I would, I tell you.'

Morgause cackled with appreciation. 'Morgan, do you know why she wouldn't take him?'

'Oh, I know,' said Morgan.

Vivian looked from one to the other, seeing only persecutors.

'It's because she's besotted with Merlin,' said Morgause. 'Old Merlin; old enough to be her father, or her grandfather. Oh yes, Granddad's darling! Perhaps he'll leave you all his money when he dies . . .' and her voice ran off into a shrill ringing laugh.

Overwrought and overtired, Vivian broke down into uncontrollable tears.

'Oh, I hate you, I hate you both,' she sobbed, 'but I hate Morgan the most.' And she ran from them, back into the woods, to seek a quiet place to weep.

Torion, after sleeping nearly the clock round, sat soberly by the door of the woodland hut, eating bread and cheese and talking to Mother Woodedge. All he could talk about was the young lady.

'Yes, that's the Lady Vivian,' Mother Woodedge

explained. 'She's a good lady, the very best. I don't know where we'd be if it wasn't for her. She saved my boy from Uther Pendragon's men, when they was after him for poaching and would have hanged him. The Pendragon is terrible hard on any that takes his deer, and we were in sore need. How she saved him I don't know. The Pendragon's men tramped right past him, where he was hid, well nigh on top of him they were, but they never seed him. Some says it's the powers she has – that she's in with those we call the Good Neighbours, not to name no names. I've seen them with her a time or two, seen them with my own eyes. But she's not a witch; no, she's no witch. Her two sisters, now they're witches, I'd say, and I'd never do aught to offend them, as I don't know what they might do. They all go and visit the witches down along in the wood from time to time, but she's not a witch, no, not the Lady Vivian.'

'But where do they come from, these ladies?'

'Why, all we know is that they're some great lord's daughters from far over northward, but more than that we don't know – and those that know mustn't tell. But she's a good lady. What she gives us in the summer sees us through the winter so's we don't starve, and she puts a blessing on the place as well, on my little milch-cow and my bees and my apple trees, and on what the dog gets in the woods. Sometimes we think she's like one of those the old tales tell about – the great ladies of the woods in times gone by. There was one they called Nimuë. They said she made the flowers grow in the spring and the beasts bring forth young.'

When the woodwife was gone, Torion sat and thought always of Vivian. In his thoughts there was never any forward-looking, never any plan of life. What would he ask of her? Not to be his bride – one has no such thoughts about a heavenly manifestation of beauty. Only to admire her, to bathe his eyes in her sight, to lose himself in contact with her . . . In bodily contact? Oh, dear God, what intoxication, perhaps to die in that moment. Even at the thought his loins stirred. Torion cleared his mind of such temptation as the woodwife returned.

'Will she come back here, do you think?' he asked.

'Why yes, in a day or a week or so, while the summer lasts.'

'Then, goodwife, would you be so kind as to let me stay here till I see her again?'

'Surely, sir, you bide here as long as you've a mind to. My son and my good man are up along in the woods, and will be for a while. I'm glad of the company, and may be you can help me with some chores. Is the heap of fern in the shippen good enough for you?'

'Oh excellent, goodwife; I ask for no better.'

'And our food's nothing much—'

'I shall not eat.'

'Oh, never say that! Don't be a fool, lad. Of course you'll eat. What good will you be to a lady if you fall over with faintness when next you see her?'

And so she coaxed him, almost forced him, to eat her good frumenty and clotted cream and eggs and butter, though he hardly knew what he did.

And on the third day he saw Vivian again, riding on a white horse. She dismounted and almost ran to him, her hands outstretched, her face aglow with delight.

'My dear friend! I had to come and see how you fared. Are you well? Mother Woodedge has looked after you?

Come, I have so much to tell you. Let us walk in the woods. No, not ride; I love to walk. Let me show you where the bluebell glades are. Have you forgotten that it is May?'

In a daze of bliss he followed her, hardly finding a word in answer. It was indeed May, and he now realized it, and tasted the beauty of the time, as she led him through it and pointed out all its charm and graces. Things he would never have noticed before – not only the bluebells, though they made a heaven of the ground they sprang from, but the first little sparks of crimson that were the campions, setting off the blue; wood anemones, and the great green trusses of the wood-spurge; late-flowering wild cherries overhead, and the blush-pink of the crab-apples; Solomon's Seal and the lilies of the valley. Enchantment after enchantment, and he saw each one as an adornment to her, and of her beauty, a new gentleness and warmth and kindness.

And at last, deep in the untrodden woods, she led him to a little dell, roofed over with the stretching boughs of beech trees, where last year's brown beech-leaves lay in a thick rustling drift. Here she stood still and, saying nothing, took off her long grey mantle and laid it on the ground. Underneath the mantle she wore only a light, translucent dress. Her arms reached out to him, and she drew him down to the beech-leaf bed.

It was late morning and the sun was high, shining through the open lattice window where the girls were sleeping. Vivian was awakened by the sound of Morgan laughing.

'What are you laughing at, Morgan?'

'Why, you, among other things. Thank you very much, dear Vivian, for the loan of your beautiful lover.'

'What do you mean?' Vivian exclaimed, jumping out of bed and looking down at Morgan, who lolled against her pillows.

'Why, dear sister, as you wouldn't take pity on the poor man, I did. There, in the woods, I took your shape and, of course, he thought I was you.'

'You didn't! Oh Morgan, you didn't, did you?'

'Indeed I did, and he enjoyed it, and so did I. You were a fool not to take your chance when you had it.'

'Morgan—' Vivian could find no words. Indignation and anger choked her. In the other bed Morgause, lying snug and listening, chuckled to herself.

'You certainly don't deserve him,' Morgan went on. 'So wrapped up in dreams of old Merlin, you couldn't take pity on a fine young fellow. Oh, he's a grand lover, I can tell you—'

'Be quiet!' cried Vivian, her cheeks crimson. 'Morgan, how could you do such a thing? I'll never speak to you again . . .'

Morgan laughed her most spiteful laugh and turned back to her pillow.

He was watching the path to the hut and, as soon as Vivian came in sight on her white horse, he ran to her, holding her stirrup as she dismounted, and would have taken her in his arms, crying, 'Oh my lady, my dear love . . .', but she slipped from his arms and put him from her, gently.

'No, my dear man, no; not like that.'

'But, my lady – after last night, surely . . . ?'

'No . . . no . . . no.' She shook her head more in frustration with herself than with him, and thrust him away with one long slim hand. 'You are mistaken.' She sighed and found it difficult to look him in the face. She tried, but looked away again as she spoke. 'It was not I, last night.'

'Not you? What do you mean?'

'It was my sister, Morgan – she took my shape.' She looked up again at Torion's yearning and puzzled face. 'Don't you understand? That was not I at all. I was not here. It was my sister, Morgan.'

He stared back at her, incredulous.

'What are you telling me? That it was not you, not you, my dear love, in my arms? Oh no, no, I can't believe it. Lady, this is a jest. You are taunting me.'

'I am not. I was not here.' She found she was shouting and she had not meant to. 'Oh, my poor friend. I have told you, I cannot give you my love, for it is given to another. I was not here, last night. It was not me . . .'

Amazement, frustration, rage followed in waves across his face.

'You are lying to me. You have deceived me. Why? Oh God, why? You were so kind, so loving to me yesterday. And now you deny that we ever . . . My love, how can you think I did not know it was you? How could I be mistaken? Your lips, your face, your beautiful body; surely, surely . . .'

His hands groped for her. She stepped back, eluding his grasp, but he followed her.

'Do not deny me. Why do you torment me so? Have I displeased you? Have you been persuaded to deny our love? Has someone . . .? You say you have another lover . . . by the flames below, if you have played me false, and in so short a time . . .'

There was a mad blaze in his eyes. He made a quick lunge forward and seized her wrist.

'Don't touch me,' she cried. 'Let me go. I have told you, I – I feel kindly to you . . .'

'*Kindly!*' he scoffed.

'I do feel kindly to you, but I do not and cannot love you. It was my sister Morgan, who is a witch . . .'

'And so are you!'

'Torion, please listen. I do not wish to hurt you. My sister Morgan took my shape and came to you yesterday. This morning she told me . . .'

'*Lies!* All lies!' He dragged on her wrist, trying to pull her close to him.

'No. Let me go . . .' She was afraid of him now. His right hand gripped her hard and his left was reaching towards her neck, her face – his eyes had a glare of madness. With a sudden effort she broke free and jumped out of range. He did not try to follow. Instead, all strength seemed to drain from him. He buried his face in his hands, and then looked up to heaven with a great cry.

'Tricked! Betrayed! Deceived!' And turning, he dashed madly away into the woods.

At first she did not dare to follow him, being afraid of his burning eyes and clutching hands. Then she grew anxious for him and tried to trace where he had gone, but could not, although she knew the woods as well as anyone could know them, but every way she went she found nothing but disappointment and frustration, and she began to recognize the signs of a stronger magic working against her. She gave it up and went back to the farmstead.

'Vivian,' said Morgan two days later.

Vivian did not reply. She could not yet bring herself to speak to Morgan.

'Vivian, I think you had better listen to what I have to say,' Morgan persisted.

'Say on then.'

'If you want to see your fine lover again, you'd better go to the foot of Chough's Crag – and go at once, before the tide comes in.'

Startled, Vivian turned to look at Morgan, wondering if some new trick was afoot.

'What do you mean?'

'What I said.'

'What have you done, Morgan? Tell me!'

'Me? I have done nothing. Anything that was done he did himself.'

Chough's Crag was known to the sisters. It was a high cliff above the sea with a sheer granite face of terrifying height. Below it were jagged rocks at low tide, and at high tide, deep swirling water and strong currents. Vivian left her horse tethered to a fence a half-mile inland – any nearer the sea was not safe – and hastened down by twisting paths to the rocky shore.

He was there. His body lay shattered and twisted on the rocks, the dead face turned to the sky. But with her Clear-Sight, Vivian could see the shadow-form of the man, standing upright above the earthly body. Tall, drooping, forlorn it stood, a dark yet tenuous shape and, as it looked at her, the eyes took fire and glowed like torches. The woman in her mortal body and the man in his ghost-body confronted each other, and behind them the sun drew towards the west, reddening the sea.

He moaned and stretched his arms towards her.

'Lady, oh lady, I am so glad you have come. Lady Vivian, my love, my eyes are cleared and now I know you told me the truth. I still love you, I love you more than ever. Stay with me, now, and do not leave.'

'I must not stay with you,' she said, and her voice was choked with tears. 'And you must not stay here. For I am still in the mortal body, but you are free from it and must go yonder,' and she pointed to the west. 'Out there I can see the Gates, and there are helpers who wait for you.'

'Where must I go?' he said, his luminous, spectral eyes full of fear. 'To Judgement – to the flames of hell?'

'No, no, dear man. Judgement there must be, and payment, no doubt, but not as you think. He is very merciful. You need not be afraid. Look. The presences in the west are kindly and helpful. Go on the shining path and be happy.'

'Then come with me. I will not go unless you do.'

'But dear Torion, I cannot come with you. I am in the body, and have to stay in my body.'

'I will not go without you.'

'You must. I cannot come.'

'I will not go from here.'

'Oh, do not be so foolish. Can you not understand? Soon the tide will come in and your poor bones that lie there will be overwhelmed by the waters. Then either you will follow them, and be tossed to and fro without rest, or you will haunt here under the cliff, in darkness and misery, until you see reason and go on your way. Why must you make yourself a miserable wraith? Go in peace where they wait for you.'

'Not without you.'

She considered, frowning, deeply troubled. Then at last she knew what to do. Since an illusion had wrecked him, an illusion should save him.

She drew one hair out of her head, long and dark-red chestnut. She held it before her, blowing in the wind. It took a shape, an outline, and as her thoughts worked upon it, the outline thickened and took form, until there stood a simulacrum of herself, perfect in every detail, even down to the least roughness of a fingernail. It spoke in her voice as she stepped back out of sight.

'Come then, my love,' it said. 'I will lead you on your way, and will not forsake you. Give me your hand and let us go into the Land of Light.'

And the ghost-body of Torion put its hand trustfully into the hand of the double of Vivian. The sun dipped and sent a long, red path across the sea on to which the two stepped. Far off the real Vivian could see, against the sun, the pillars of the Golden Gates, and beyond them certain tall, solemn presences. Torion would be safe.

The tide was coming in. She laid the limbs of Torion's earthly body straight and seemly, with his hands crossed over his breast, though she knew the sea would not leave them so for long, and she sprinkled sand for earth, and made the sign of the Holy Cross over the body.

She took one last look towards the horizon and fancied she saw the shapes of two lovers, and then she went home in the twilight and wept bitterly as she rode.

PART II

The King That Shall Be

1. Something Brewing

Time passed, and the three girls were sixteen. Merlin grew older, indeed he seemed to age quickly, as if he had cares of which they knew nothing. His hair and beard were plentifully powdered with grey and his face was lined. He was often away from Tintagel. After one long absence he returned with a white headcloth instead of green, and with a little leather bag hanging round his neck, as if it hid a jewel, but he would not let the girls see what it contained. They noticed too that he wore a strange ring of bronze, set with a great green stone. But he would not let them touch that either, not even Vivian.

They all progressed well at their studies. Their big schoolroom at the top of the tower had four recessed windows in the corners, deep enough for a chair, a book-rest on the window-ledge, and little shelves and cupboards fitted against the embrasure. Each girl had one of these, and Merlin had the fourth. Their laboratories, he called them, or working places. Here each girl kept her own collection of herbs, gums, spices, extracts, all sorts of things – lumps of ambergris from the sea, scraps of mummia from the dead bodies of Egyptian kings, skins and bones of birds and small beasts, pieces of earth and metals, as well as retorts and alembics, stills and crucibles, and a few rare, handwritten books. In those little laboratories, each of the three sisters made her own magic.

Among other things, Merlin taught them the arts of the healer. He was himself in great demand among the people of the castle and in the scattered villages on the mainland. As the girls grew more expert he would often take them with him when he visited the sick. Vivian had a natural aptitude and loved the work of healing. Her presence was encouraging to sick folk, and they were all convinced that a healing virtue went out from her and helped them. Morgan, on the other hand, was nothing but a discourager. People grew afraid of her and requested Merlin not to bring her. She professed to be so bored that nothing could relieve the tedium but the practice of little cruelties on the sly. Merlin was kept busy detecting and undoing her mischief.

Morgause showed a special aptitude for midwifery and was always to be found where there was a woman in labour. She made an efficient midwife, surprisingly attentive and gentle, but always more interested in the child than the mother. When the child was born, if it was a boy, she would hang over it, gloat over it almost, calling it her baby brother. The mothers grew alarmed at her uncanny, intense brooding over the little boys – the way she would clasp and fondle them, and hardly give them out of her hands to their mothers'. Some of the women would eye her askance, and mutter prayers, and even make the sign against the evil eye. Merlin would click his tongue and afterwards hint to Duke Gorlais that it was time his daughters were married, Morgause in particular. Yet Morgause showed no interest in the young men around the castle, only in the babies.

Soon Morgause was sent for by the Duchess and rather solemnly told that a marriage had been arranged for her with King Lot of Orkney. She listened indifferently, and did not seem to care much. She did not even ask if he were young or old, comely or ugly, kind or tyrannous. She accepted what was coming to her, without interest. Her sisters, and the nurses, were much more interested.

'And so now, young mistress,' said Olwen La Nourrice, 'you will have sons of your own.'

'I don't want sons,' she replied sullenly. 'I want a baby brother.'

'Oh you'll have sons for all that,' said Olwen. 'And like it. You'd better.'

Morgause flounced across the castle garden where they were talking.

'Olwen – *why* doesn't my mother give me a baby brother?'

'Oh, ask no questions and you'll be told no lies,' was all that Olwen would say.

Olwen strode away with conscious dignity, the black veil on her hennin fluttering behind her. Morgause and the other two turned back into the smaller rose garden. All around them the high walls kept off the rough wind from the sea. Beyond the walls nothing would grow but sea-pinks and samphire. Here, among the roses, was one of the other nurses, Gwen, Vivian's personal woman, much more approachable than Olwen.

'Gwen,' said Morgause, as Gwen clipped and culled the roses, 'why does my mother not have any more children?

I mean, I know well enough what is required for a woman to have a child – God knows I've delivered a score or more here and in the village – but our mother is still young, and our father – he's a good man . . .'

Gwen buried her head deeper into the roses.

'Perhaps, young mistress . . . oh well, if you must know, perhaps he's *too* good a man.'

'What do you mean?'

'Well, there's good and there's good. There's what a priest would call good, and there's good in other ways. You must know how devout my Lord Gorlais has become these days.'

'Why, yes, we're always being called into chapel when he's home from fighting Uther Pendragon . . .'

'You see – he comes home from fighting, and he goes into the chapel, he greets my lady very courteously, and then . . .' She looked back towards the castle behind them, with its two great towers. '. . . And then you and my lady remain here, in this part of the castle, and my lord and his men go off to that part, and very soon he's off to the wars again. You don't get babies that way.'

'Oh, I see,' said Morgause.

'Mind you, if it were me, I don't think I'd complain,' said Gwen. 'A woman has enough troubles. But not all of them have the sense to see it. I think, madame, your mother is content enough.'

Morgause sighed and went off shaking her head.

'What are you doing?' Morgan asked as she and Vivian came up behind Morgause in her little 'laboratory'.

'Making something,' said Morgause without turning round. She was bent over an assortment of pots and jars, glasses, tongs and spoons; and propped up before her was a book.

'Making what?' Vivian stole a glimpse over her shoulder.

'Oh, no matter,' mocked Morgan. 'No need to make such a mystery. I know what you're making.'

'No you don't!' exclaimed Morgause, taking her gaze for an instant off her work and turning her head. Vivian thrust a glance over her shoulder and stole a look at the book.

'Oh Morgause, it's a love charm,' Vivian exclaimed. 'And out of Merlin's little book, too, the one he won't let us see. Morgause, he didn't let you have it, did he?'

'Of course he did,' said Morgause, with the smirk she always put on when lying.

'That's a lie,' said Morgan. (It's not easy to tell lies, Morgause had reflected on previous occasions, when both your sisters have the Clear-Sight.)

'Well then—' she admitted. 'What if I did take it? I'll put it back before he knows.'

'But he never lets us make up love potions,' said Vivian.

'Who's to tell him? You?' Morgause turned round. 'I tell you, if either of you says a word to him about it, I'll blast you both with the palsy, by the Goddess, I will!'

'Oh, no, no . . .' Vivian assured her.

'You know me better than that,' Morgan said.

'But who's it for?' said Vivian.

'It's none of your business. Why, it might be for anyone where it would come in handy.' Very composedly she poured what she had brewed into a small glass bottle and sealed it up.

'So long as it isn't for one of us,' said Morgan.

'Oh, you never know,' Morgause taunted. 'I doubt it would work on you, Morgan. You're not human enough. And it would be wasted on Vivian.' Morgan looked pleased by the comment, whilst Vivian fired red. 'Who knows?' Morgause continued. 'I might want it for my wedding with this King Lot, whoever he is.'

She stowed the bottle away carefully in a small cupboard which she locked with a key that she carried on a bracelet, and then strutted out of the room, leaving the others to their thoughts.

2. Noble Guest

There was excitement in the castle of Tintagel. After all these years of warfare, Uther Pendragon was coming in peace. Neither side had yielded to the other. It would seem that they had simply fought each other into the ground and were tired of it. Uther Pendragon was to be a peaceful guest in the castle.

The girls were full of curiosity. What kind of man was he, that their father had been fighting for so long? What did he look like? Not much older than the Duke, they had heard, and a sufficiently goodly man.

'You must wear your best dresses and your jewellery,' said the Duchess. 'Who knows – his wife is dead, and with Morgause provided for, he might take a liking to one of you. They say he's a fine man. One of you must bring the loving-cup. Which one?'

Oh please, not me, said Vivian to herself. The idea frightened her, and anyway, for her there was no man in the world but Merlin.

'You, Morgan?'

'Oh no, not for my humour,' said Morgan, turning her head over her fine ivory-white shoulder. 'You know you'd say afterwards that my look had turned it sour.'

'Why, I do believe it would. Oh well, it will have to be Morgause, though she's the betrothed one.'

'Oh, I'm willing,' said Morgause, dimpling. 'Now, what do I do?'

'Just hand the cup to your father first, with a curtsey. Then to our guest and then to me.'

'Nobody else?'

'No, nobody else.'

'Don't I get a drink of it?'

'No.'

Morgause gave a peevish grunt at that, but it seemed to Vivian that she was not at all displeased, not by any means.

The guest was below in the great hall. They could hear his booming voice. In the bower, the intimate little room that opened off the dais of the great hall, Morgause was preparing the loving-cup. It was a large, two-handed vessel of very precious silver, set with gems. A fine embroidered napkin was looped round one handle. Morgause was carefully filling the great cup with a heady mixture of metheglin and white wine. Vivian looked over her shoulder. Morgause was mixing something else in with it as well. Vivian could see that she was concealing a little bottle in her hand.

'Morgause!' She was almost too appalled to speak. 'What *are* you doing? What is that you've put in it? You wouldn't dare—'

'Oh yes I would,' Morgause rejoined coolly. 'To make

something happen at last. There's Mother and Father and this stranger . . . something's bound to happen.'

Morgan, listening, stood by with an enigmatic smile. She said: 'All I ask, sister dear, is that you've mixed it right. It contains, if I remember rightly, two deadly poisons, one balanced against the other. Too bad if you haven't measured them correctly . . .'

'Oh Morgause, you wouldn't,' Vivian cried. 'Not our mother . . .' Not that she felt very deeply attached to her mother, whom they seldom saw, but she was their mother all the same, and Vivian suddenly saw her as vulnerable, and therefore appealing. She should not be put at risk.

'What's all this noise?' The Duchess parted the curtains and came into the room, a striking figure, tall and dark-haired, her eyes bright with excitement. Gorlais followed her, a long-faced man, dark, like many Cornishmen, black-bearded and black-browed, not fierce, but rather mild and gentle. He offered Ygraine his arm with a fine ceremonial gesture as they went through the curtain-covered doorway on to the dais, where Uther Pendragon awaited them. The daughters followed behind. Morgause brought the loving-cup, and Morgan and Vivian followed together, just behind. Vivian was trembling, clutching her hands at her sides.

There stood the formidable Uther Pendragon, king (some said usurper) and war-leader of all of southern Britain. A tall man, more solid than Gorlais, with fine blond hair and beard, the colour of ripe corn, which glowed in his broad face.

All was ceremony and state, with curtseying and kissing of hands. They paraded in the wide open space in front of the table, below the dais, the men-at-arms of both parties stood together with cups filled, to drink to amity and peace. Ygraine stepped back a little and led Morgause forward with the brimming cup. Despite her plumpness, Morgause looked resplendent, her luxuriant blonde hair complemented by a flowing dress of midnight blue.

She took the cup first to her father.

'I pledge you my friendship, Uther Pendragon,' he said lifting the cup in a toast, 'and I would indeed drink with you, but this is Lent and a Friday, and I am also under a vow. But my lady will drink with you, and I touch the cup to my lips as a token.' He did so and wiped the cup with a napkin, passing it back to Morgause. A frown of vexation passed over Morgause's face as she took the cup and bore it to Uther.

'Health and peace to all here,' he said in his loud, booming voice, 'and to you, my good Gorlais of Cornwall, and to my beautiful hostess, your lady.' He took the cup firmly and drank deep of it. The eyes of the three girls were on him all the time. Then Morgause carried the cup to Ygraine.

Vivian could bear it no longer.

'Mother, no!' she whispered urgently.

'Quiet, child,' said the Duchess, and set the cup to her lips, sipping lightly.

Vivian's dismay and despair overcame her. 'Don't drink it, Mother, please don't.'

'Child, remember your manners, and be quiet.' She raised the cup to her lips again.

There was only one thing to do. Vivian recalled her skills of illusion.

'Mother,' she whispered, 'don't you see, there's a slug in the cup.'

And before Ygraine's horrified eyes there arose a slug, black and green and slimy, bubbling up out of the wine. The goblet slipped from Ygraine's hands and splashed at her feet, the spilled wine flooding the carpet of the dais. Ygraine, with a handkerchief to her mouth, choking on some incoherent words, stumbled back into the room behind, one of the maids quickly following her and closing the curtains.

Gorlais turned to Uther, his sallow face tinged pink with embarrassment.

'My Lord Uther, I do apologize. I beg you will forgive this mishap, a mischance. Women, you know . . .'

But Uther seemed rapt in a dream.

'My good Gorlais, no need, no need. Your lady, indeed, my Lord Gorlais, she is altogether admirable. Never have I seen a lovelier lady. Come now, think nothing of this little mishap.'

Vivian stood before them stammering. 'My Lord Uther, my mother begs you will excuse her and by all means begin the feast without her.'

'Let us do so, Gorlais my friend,' said Uther. 'But I hope we shall see the Lady Ygraine at some future time for, by the Old Gods, she is the very paragon of beauty.'

The feast went on, the two lords absorbed in each other's company, the three girls all on edge – Morgan inclined to laugh, Morgause watching Uther as if awaiting the result of an experiment, Vivian trembling and unable to eat. The moment they were able to leave the board, with elaborate curtseys as required, Vivian hastened through the curtains into the bower, the other two pressing close behind her. The Duchess had retired.

'How is she?' Vivian asked breathlessly of nurse Gwen. 'Did she cast up?'

'Oh no, she didn't puke,' Gwen replied bluntly. 'She's too self-commanded for that, being a lady. Now, if it had been me—!'

'So?' said Morgause, with her infuriating smile. 'So, some of the potion remains in her, in spite of you, you meddling marplot . . .' and she turned angrily on Vivian.

Vivian rounded upon her. 'Morgause, what have you done? Don't you realize, if the least thing had gone wrong with your potion, you could have poisoned our mother.'

'My potions don't go wrong,' said Morgause.

'And now what have you done? What's to happen?'

'We shall wait and see,' said Morgause. 'As to what I've done – Merlin said I was to be an instrument in the hands of Destiny.'

'*Merlin* said!' This came as a shock to Vivian. 'Oh no, he never told you to . . .'

'I did not say he told me what to do. But he knew, and that is what he said.'

Morgan, standing behind, was laughing softly to herself. Vivian turned on her.

'And you – what are you laughing at?'

'Oh, never mind, you worryguts. Perhaps I'm laughing about Morgause and that baby brother she wants so much. What she'll do to get him, and yet he's to be my enemy.'

It was Morgause's turn to confront Morgan.

'What do you mean? If you dare to hurt him when he's here, I'll send the ten-legged spider after you.'

Morgan found it increasingly hysterical. 'I won't be able to harm him, not myself. But *you*, my dear sister, oh yes, you'll get him, and have him, and possess him, and ruin him. No one but you.' The last word was spat viciously into Morgause's face and then, as the look of astonishment increased, Morgan burst out laughing again.

All that night the revel went on. The men from both armies caroused happily in the big hall, and on the dais Uther Pendragon drank and talked and drank and talked, while Gorlais, keeping his vow, sat with an empty cup, sober and morose, listening while Uther extolled the beauties of his lovely wife.

3. Terms of Peace

So peace was concluded between Gorlais and Uther Pendragon, and the whole countryside could breathe more quietly. The family of the Duke was invited to a Whitsun revel at Uther's great fortress. Great were the rejoicings, for even Gorlais's private army, tough men who thought time wasted when it was not spent fighting, were a little tired of the long campaign, especially against men of their own kin. It had continued for far too long, and done too much damage. They would be glad of a rest, and a pleasant summer, and then perhaps they would join with Uther's men to push back some of those yellow-haired, red-faced seafarers who kept coming over and taking land. It would be good sense to stand together with Uther's men, whom they had found very worthy, even as enemies, to make an efficient army to repel the foreigners.

The three princesses were thrilled. New dresses were made for them, beautiful dresses made of 'cloth of Athens', or satin, so glossy and supple and in such lovely colours. Deep crimson, like plum juice, for Morgan, rose-pink for Morgause, and light luminous green for Vivian; and for their mother, white, richly encrusted with silver embroidery. She was in a strange state, half uplifted, half tremulous, sometimes finding all sorts of reasons why they couldn't go, or why she personally couldn't go, and then other times full of anticipation. A lesser woman would have been giggling, but with her it was a kind of sparkle, which from minute to minute she would lose and fall silent and breathless, as if afraid.

She made a great show of her hope to make a match between Uther and Vivian.

'Oh no, Mother,' protested Vivian. 'Not me. I . . . I don't want to be married.'

'Nonsense, child.'

'Anyway, he's too old.'

'He's not as old as Merlin,' Morgan interposed spitefully. For it was quite plain to all that Vivian's heart was set on Merlin. The seed of doubt that Morgause had sown in her mind by declaring that Merlin had spoken of Morgause as an instrument of Destiny would not die, and troubled her mind. Could Merlin also be of that sinister conspiracy, of which the threads, like drifting gossamers, floated always around Morgan and Morgause; and what about Olwen and the witch-queen?

Merlin had been away for several months in the north country and had seen nothing of Uther's visit. When he returned on a warm, tense evening in April, when the sea and the sky were smooth, still and waiting, Vivian stepped out before any of the others, and walked up the narrow causeway that joins Tintagel to the land. On a rough day, a man in armour could be blown off that causeway – but this evening no wind stirred and the rosy sky hid its horizon in a blue haze; the waves lapped quietly.

Merlin, in his white robe and head-coif with the gold

tribann over his forehead, rode a black horse, and some four or five of the Duke's servants attended him. He was looking older, his neat little black beard was spreading and bushy, with traces of grey. A lock or two of silver-tinged hair escaped from under the white coif. There were two deep furrows between his eyes. To Vivian he was immortal.

Her face glowed with pleasure as he greeted her, and he dismounted and clasped her hands warmly. She led him away from the servants.

'Merlin, oh Merlin,' she exclaimed in obvious anxiety. 'Tell me this at once. Did you tell Morgause to give our mother the love potion?'

He looked at her searchingly.

'What makes you think I did?'

'Oh Merlin, don't equivocate. I couldn't bear it if you lied to me.'

He laid his hand tenderly on her shoulder.

'There should be no lies between us. I tell you true. Morgause needed no telling from me. But you may say that I knew she would do it.'

'But she said you told her to be an instrument in the hand of Destiny. Did you, did you?'

'Dear child, no one can tell another to be an instrument of Destiny. Destiny chooses its own tools. But what I said to her was that I knew she might prove to be an instrument in the hands of Destiny. Be sure I never told her what to do, though I knew full well she would do it, and I know now that she has done it.'

Vivian relaxed and fell into step beside him on the narrow path. She bent her head and he passed his hand over her smooth, red-gold hair.

'Vivian. I will also have my part to play – a difficult, dark and perilous part. Can you trust me to do what is best and of most value for Britain and for Christendom?'

He drew her round to face him.

'Do you trust me, Vivian?'

From a full-hearted impulse, she answered.

'I love you.'

The servants had gone ahead; there was no one to see them now. Merlin bent his face over her head, his hands caressing the stray shining tendrils of red hair.

'Oh Vivian, little Vivian, do you indeed? Vivian, what have I done? What must I yet do to you? Dare I? Must I lay such a fate upon you, sweet child of gentle, smiling Nature? Can I, in all conscience . . . ? Oh, Vivian, sweet, lovely child, little do you know . . .'

Fearlessly she looked up at him, and said, 'Lay what fate upon me you must. I am willing.'

And, looking at him, she saw a change. A white light shone through his face. His hair was white, white as the oldest of old men, but shot through with silver. His eyebrows, his beard, every part of his face was radiating, vibrant, and in the midst, his blue eyes, like the sea.

'I am willing,' she repeated.

Slowly the light ebbed from his face.

'My dear, you make it too easy for me. I am not what I seem. I am older than you think; far, far older. The roots of my being are deeper than I can tell you. But you have a part in that great lineage – you and the others.'

'Morgan?' she said, trembling, her face overshadowed with fear.

'Morgan is as old as I am. She was, long before the body she now wears, as I was also. Where I am white, she is black. She and I are adversaries, and will be to the end of time. Beware of her.'

'And Morgause?'

'Morgause is sensual, lazy, selfish. She stands idly between the black and the white, and because she follows her appetites, she will drift off towards the dark. But she also, as she said, and as I said, is the instrument of Destiny. That baby brother that she desires so much, he is foretold and destined.' Vivian hastened to ask more, but Merlin laid a finger on her lips. 'Oh, I cannot tell you yet, but far, far ahead lies his path among the stars: he is destined to be greater than all of us.'

'And I? What of me, Merlin?'

'You are all of the Light, and you will not turn to the Dark. You are of the sweet earth, when she is yet Ceridwen Cariad-wen. And so, God forgive me, I must use you. You must be the Lady of the Lake, and your name shall be Nimuë.'

'I am willing,' she said again. 'But you will not let them marry me to Uther Pendragon?'

'To Uther Pendragon? No, the Gods forbid! Never to Uther Pendragon, although . . . But no matter. Be content. Uther Pendragon will not choose you. At least you can thank Morgause for that.'

Whitsuntide had come, a time of high revelry and pleasant weather. The cavalcade set off from Tintagel, all in glittering array, with flags flying and banners streaming; the fine ladies upon their white horses, all tinkling and sparkling, to visit Uther Pendragon at his court at Castle Orgulous.

Only Vivian went with a heavy heart. Ygraine had

impressed upon her, over and over again, that the Pendragon was to ask her in marriage, in order to seal the peace and unite the two warring tribes, and that she must not refuse. She tried to comfort her mind with Merlin's assurance that Uther would not choose her. She exerted all she knew of mental magic as she went along, repeating to herself words of power and reiterating, as if she saw it written before her: *Uther Pendragon will not ask for my hand*. Merlin was not there. His mysterious comings and goings had taken him away once more. Vivian felt helpless without him. There was nothing she could do but repeat her spells and affirmations. The blooming countryside, as they passed through it, full of foaming hawthorn and long meadows of scabious, blue, purple and pink, was dark and colourless to her, and the sun shone in vain.

They were all made very welcome at Castle Orgulous. The three girls had never seen such richness: simple enough, actually, but far above anything the narrow boundaries of Tintagel had ever seen. Fresh scented rushes on all the floors, carpets spread over the tables, for each lady a bower all to herself, enclosed with boards of fragrant timber; beds of down instead of piles of sheepskins; cups and jugs of bronze and silver and gilt. Down the length of the hall flambeaux burned in metal sconces with a white light, and illumined the richly coloured pictures on the walls.

The pageant of welcome was over, and next came the feast. The tables overflowed with food and wine. Morgause could not believe her eyes, but remembered that she was a guest and retained her decorum throughout the evening. The meal drew to its close, though the drinking went on, but the important moment was now at hand. On the great dais, at the two ends of the table, the two chiefs faced one another – Gorlais, dark and pale, his long black hair hanging limply each side of his face, his dark eyes dull and hooded; and Uther, red-faced, square-shouldered, flushed with wine and full of the greatness of himself and the occasion. There advanced up the steps two solemn men in black robes, with scrolls of parchment, followed by an attendant with inkhorns and quill pens – the clerks who were to write the terms of peace. From behind the dais the sound of a horn cut through the babel of voices. Behind Gorlais, his lady and three daughters stood close and expectant.

'Listen, all ye present,' began the Pendragon in his great voice, and he proceeded to tell them that peace was now concluded between the two peoples that had been at war so long, that the borders between Cornwall and Britain should be thus-and-thus, and the people's rights be such-and-such, and that henceforward they should be as one in keeping back the Saxon invaders.

'And in token and surety thereof,' the Pendragon continued, as the scribes scratched away busily, 'we think it is proper to unite the two lands by a good marriage, that I myself shall take a wife amongst those whom we have fought for so long.'

A cheer went up from the folk in the hall below the dais. Gorlais led Vivian out, her red hair and pale green dress gleaming, though her face was white.

'My Lord Pendragon,' he said formally, 'you do me honour. I hereby offer you my daughter, the Princess Vivian of Tintagel.' And he took her cold hand and extended it towards Uther. Yet Uther did not take it.

'I thank you, my Lord Gorlais,' he said, 'but I do not choose this lady, beauteous and charming though she is.'

An angry growl came from the benches where the Duke of Cornwall's men were seated.

'Nor any of your daughters, beautiful though they all are,' Uther continued. 'You have another in your gift who far surpasses them. Give me your own wife, the Duchess Ygraine.'

Now it was a gasp of astonishment and dismay that came from the Cornish tables. The Pendragon's men made no sound, but waited. Ygraine, brilliant in her white dress, stepped forward, fearless with indignation, her cheeks blazing.

'My Lord Pendragon,' she said so that all in the hall heard her, 'you forget yourself. I am my Lord Gorlais's wife, and a husband does not barter his wife away. Take back what you have said, or there will be much regret.'

She turned to Gorlais for his support; indeed, she expected him to start forward with his hand on his sword, but he did not. He hesitated, and stood dumb.

'Come, my lady, and my lord,' the Pendragon continued, no less defiant than before. 'Those are my terms. That is the condition of peace. It is your choice, but I may tell you that, without your hand, my lady, there shall be no peace between us.'

Gorlais looked from the one to the other, and found his voice at last.

'My Lord Pendragon, what you ask is very . . . difficult. I have offered you my daughter . . .'

'Difficult!' cried Ygraine with bitter dismay.

'I have said I will not have your daughter,' said Uther,

bluntly. 'I will have the Lady Ygraine, or there is no peace between us.'

Gorlais still hesitated. Then Ygraine swung her long-sleeved arm in front of her, scattering the cups on the board.

'You!' she cried to Gorlais. 'I am to be bought and sold between you, like a beast?'

'No, no, my beloved wife,' protested Gorlais, but too tardily and seemingly more with a tone of frustration than respect.

'My lady,' said Uther, 'do not mistake me. I love and desire you above all else in this world, and so I must have you.' And his ardent eyes dwelt on her face.

'You brought me here to insult me,' she retorted. 'Come, daughters, let us go from this place.' She swept from the dais, driving the three girls before her, and calling for her attendants. Although it was night, she would not stay one moment, but ordered the servants to saddle up and be ready to leave.

'Well then,' said Uther to Gorlais, 'there can be no peace between us.' He threw his sword down on the table. 'I give you and your men till daylight to depart from here and after that it shall be war between us, as before.'

From beyond the door they could hear the jingling bridles as the Duchess and her personal retinue departed.

Gorlais roused himself. 'My Lord Pendragon – if you attempt to pursue my lady, I and my men will thin your ranks before we die.'

'Be content, Gorlais, be content. None of my men shall stir from here till daybreak. Your lady shall return to Tintagel. After that, let the storm break. Be assured that I shall find the means to attain what I desire.'

'It is thus,' spat Gorlais, 'that things are done in a Christian land?'

'Christian!' laughed Uther Pendragon.

Meanwhile, through the dark the four ladies, muffled in black mantles, which the wind kept twitching, rode in the midst of their escort, Ygraine seething with anger and pride – and yet, with a kind of exultant glow. Vivian, keeping close by her, was sick with fear, and she was sure she could hear Morgan and Morgause laughing together behind her.

4. Who Goes There?

So began for the three sisters what was a time of uncertainty and fear: the siege of Tintagel. Uther had given Gorlais fair warning that he would 'stuff him and garnish him'. Gorlais gave his steward, an old knight called Drusus, orders on his behalf to see that the castle was sufficiently full of provisions to withstand a long siege. On that fateful night, Gorlais had ridden after Ygraine and her daughters, and made as if to go with them back to Tintagel, but Ygraine had rounded on him and forbidden him to accompany them.

'Go back,' she said, sitting on her horse in the middle of the road. 'I don't need you with me; I can look after myself.'

'But my dear lady wife, I must protect you . . .'

'Protect me! You could not even stand up to Uther. You as nearly as anything consented to giving me to him. A man who was a man would have dashed his cup in his face. Why did you hesitate? A man who was a man! Yet you talk of protecting me. Go back. You'll do better to hold your other castle against Uther, at Terrabil. It bars his road to Tintagel. If you go there and hold it, it will give me time to get to Tintagel. But why should I have to tell you this? The craft of war about which I should know nothing. Call yourself a soldier! Get back, and hold Terrabil, while I furnish Tintagel for a siege.'

He had never seen her like this before. In the dark he gave a great sigh, turned his horse and led his followers away, while Ygraine and her cavalcade cantered away into the night. They would have little enough time to reach Tintagel by daybreak, unless Gorlais had the sense to stop Uther at Terrabil.

Tintagel was duly provisioned and made defensible. Waggon-loads of foodstuffs were brought in from the countryside and stocked in the great store-rooms. Cattle were driven in and penned in the stockades below the walls and their byres were stocked as much as possible with last year's hay. It was the worst time for a siege, as the year's harvest was still a summer away, and the fruits were only starting to bud in the orchards. Fortunately there was wine a-plenty, and water from the castle well, and sufficient grain in the granary for bread, but the meals would soon become monotonous in their similarity if the siege lasted too long. Morgause, who spent some hours surveying the provender, rapidly became depressed until she remembered a hoard of jams and honey that had been stashed away in the pantry. When she found these she also came across a stash of dried fruits from the previous summer, and suddenly things did not seem quite so bad. Dame Olwen, however, was quick to admonish Morgause when she found her dipping her spoon in the honey.

'Think of that spoonful as your last, my young lady, as one day it may well be.'

Vivian was as depressed as Morgause, but for an entirely different reason. Although she was delighted that Uther had not accepted her as his wife, she was deeply concerned at the train of events and wished that Merlin was by her side to comfort her and advise her. He would know what to do, if only he was there, but where was he? A rumour reached the castle that Merlin had gone to Gorlais's aid at Terrabil, and though this thrilled Vivian to know that Merlin was nearby, she became concerned for his safety. The same rumour told that Castle Terrabil was closely surrounded by Uther's forces, but there was no further news.

The days and nights grew hotter and more oppressive. The atmosphere was building up for a thunderstorm, but still it did not break. The three girls had walked down to the rocky path that ran round the castle to the west, the same place where they had seen the sea-people many years before. Most often the strong winds from the south-west made it impossible for anyone to go there, but this evening there was no wind. The sea was silken smooth, the warm air oppressive, the waves made no sound other than a soft hushing trickle. Breathless in the heat they watched the sun go down, gorgeous in crimson and orange. The broad glowing circle dipped, spilling its tide of red over the sea; it burned on the edge of the horizon and was gone. Then Vivian spoke into the silence.

'I'm cold,' she said. 'Oh God, suddenly I'm cold. As cold as ice,' and she shivered.

'Oh nonsense,' said Morgause. 'Vivian, you *can't* be cold – not in this heat.'

'But I am,' said Vivian, as the sky changed from crimson to slate-blue. 'I'm freezing. Feel my hands. It's . . . it's like death. Oh my God, it is Death.'

'Whose death?' asked Morgause in disbelief.

'Father's,' she said. Behind her Morgan laughed.

'Don't laugh, Morgan. It's true, I know it now. He's dead.' She looked round at her sisters, her eyes blurred with tears and nodded violently. 'He's dead.' She pulled her shawl about her as a sea-wind rose up. Shuddering, as in a fever, she climbed back up the path to the warmth of the castle. The other two stayed looking out to sea; then they glanced at each other – and smiled. Suddenly, it was night.

In the east the thundercloud brewed. These same clouds had been building for days, but still there was no rain. The heat increased. The three girls lay uneasily on their beds in the tower chamber. Their four great windows stood unshuttered to catch the slightest movement of the breeze, but none came.

'Nearly midnight,' sighed Morgause, 'and I haven't slept yet. This is a fey night. Why, Vivian, are you *still* cold? You must have a fever.'

Vivian lay with a rug clutched over her, staring out into the darkness.

'Listen,' she said, 'someone's coming.'

'Must be miles away, then,' replied Morgause. 'I hear nothing. Morgan, what do *you* make of it – this strange night?'

For answer, from the darkest corner of the room, Morgan laughed quietly.

'They're nearer,' said Vivian. Then she rose from her

bed, put on a thick robe, and went out. The others followed. They went out to the gallery and stood there, looking over the gatehouse to the causeway. Three still figures, they stood there in the moonless dark – Morgan and Morgause in their white nightgowns, which the windless air hardly stirred; Vivian still with her dark hooded mantle clutched over her. Above them a single flash of broad sheet-lightning flared and was gone.

In that flash Vivian saw figures approaching along the causeway, still some way off. Three horsemen, but coming without clatter, without jingle of harness, stealthily, as if perhaps their horses' hooves had been muffled. To the girls' surprise they could see the wooden drawbridge being lowered, though no hail had come from the guardroom to the gatehouse. The three riders crossed the bridge and advanced. One tall knight in front, behind him another knight, and a cloaked figure, at the sight of which Vivian's heart leapt, for it was surely Merlin. Somewhere in the distance came a low rumble of thunder.

Then a sound below drew her attention to the courtyard. There was Ygraine, alone, walking quickly and quietly across the open space towards the gatehouse. She was wrapped in a cloak, but the glowing ribbons were visible, even in the moonless darkness.

Ygraine had been wakened by the lightning flash, though no sound of thunder reached her. Almost as if sleep-walking, she rose from her bed, put on her scarlet mantle and went down the stairs. It was only as she opened the door that the thunder sounded. The power of the coming storm stirred her hair, making it bristle and flare out around her head. As she put her hands to it, it crackled. Her whole body felt tense and quivering.

The quickest way to the courtyard was through the great hall, but there the squires and fighting men slept on the rushes. None could reach the ladies' bowers without rousing them. But there was a little postern gate at the foot of the turret, to which only the Duchess had the key. This she unlocked, leaving it swinging open, and stepped into the courtyard, crossing it with quick, determined steps. Three men, dismounted, were coming in through the gatehouse, silently and unannounced. The sudden swirling wind that comes before a thunderstorm accompanied them. One was Merlin, one a knight she knew distantly as a friend, and one was Gorlais.

Gorlais!

As he came towards her she felt that a miracle had happened. This was Gorlais, but somehow transfigured – glowing, ardent, like the man who had won her so impetuously, eighteen years ago, before the long blight of indifference and world-weariness and coldness had set in. Before his heart had frozen. How often she had longed and prayed in her lonely bed for the man she knew to come back to her, from the dark limbo where his spirit wandered. And here, incredibly, he was – Gorlais as she had loved him, warm and loving and full of life.

'Oh, my lord, my love!' she cried, as he held out his arms as he had not done for years, and she sank against him, nestling into his enveloping warmth.

The other two men said no word, but stole away into the shadows of the gatehouse.

'Dearest,' he said, 'I am here in secret and I must be away before daylight. Let nobody know I am here. But I could stay away no longer, my dearest and sweetest love.'

She led him through the postern gate. At that moment the storm broke and the lightning illuminated them.

Up above, on the gallery, the girls watched them till they disappeared. Then they turned and went back to their own turret chamber. From its southern window they could see the opposite tower where the Duchess had her apartments. Small slit windows marked the spiral stair inside the tower, and the girls could see the light of a taper going past each window in turn, until the rain suddenly unleashed a curtain between them and the storm broke at last.

'They've gone up together,' said Morgause, soft and tense. 'For years he hasn't. Oh I shall have him, at last, my baby brother.'

Vivian peered out, gripping the stone ledge. As she turned she saw the other two, now both taller than she, standing together and towering over her. In the hush that followed a peal of thunder, she spoke against the hiss of the rain.

'That's not Father. That wasn't the Duke Gorlais. I know a glamour when I see one.'

'We know,' said Morgan, and both she and Morgause laid their forefingers on their lips, exchanging glances above Vivian's head.

'But who is it?' cried Vivian.

'Need you ask?' Morgan replied.

'And that's your Merlin's doing,' gloated Morgause.

A heaven-rending crash drowned Vivian's reply. The flash that went with it showed Morgause grovelling on her bed with her hands to her ears. The storm-wind swept hangings and curtains before it, and blew out tapers and torches.

'Come on, shut that window,' cried Morgan. 'Magic won't help us do that.' Vivian ran to help her struggle with the shutters.

'But there's magic here,' Vivian shouted in her ear.

'I know. Strong magic. I can't oppose it. Someone is coming from the North – my most welcome enemy.'

The next day dawned sweet, clear and calm. The earth was washed and refreshed, the sea serene, as if there had been no storm. Nor was there any trace of the midnight visitors. It might all have been a dream.

Ygraine walked quietly and happily into the rose garden. The storm had done some damage, but the sunshine was bringing back the beauty. Hollyhocks, being tall, had suffered the worst, and many of them were broken or leaning. Lilies too lay flattened. Ygraine stopped and straightened one or two as she went. The roses had bowed to the storm and, though many had been scattered, new buds were opening. Ygraine moved along, happily alone, pondering over the strange and wonderful night. Gorlais, her restored lover, had left her before daybreak, as he had said he would. She had heard him ride away with Merlin and their other companion. Then she had slept.

As she mused she heard a maidservant running along the path.

'Madame, there's a messenger here.'

'A messenger? Well, let him in.'

The messenger came into the garden like a black blot against a bright picture. He was cloaked and hooded like a monk, all in dusty black. He was breathless and pale.

'My lady—'

'What is it, good man?'

'Oh, my lady, forgive me for bringing ill news . . .'

'Ill news?' She put out her hand for the maidservant and groped her way to a stone seat. The girl quickly pulled off her own cloak and spread it on the stone. Ygraine sat and turned to the messenger.

'Please tell me your news.'

'My lord, your husband, the Duke Gorlais . . .'

'Yes?'

'He is dead, my lady. Slain as he made a sortie out from Castle Terrabil.'

The bright garden swam before her.

'But when, man, when was this?'

'Last night, my lady, just at sunset.'

'At sunset? Last night . . . ? Oh God – then, who . . . ?'

And she fell into the maid's arms in a dead faint.

5. Child of the Storm

Slowly the dark procession crossed the causeway. Strung out in a line above the grey and ruffling sea they looked, from a distance, like a string of black beads, a black rosary. But nearer, they were a long frieze of black silhouettes.

First came a herald with a flag of truce. Next came monks, two by two, singing the dirge. Then the bearers, carrying between them Gorlais, a long sad shape, covered with a pall of purple and silver. Then more monks, with a cross and censers and holy water. Behind them came Uther Pendragon himself, in robes of mourning, bareheaded, his helm under his arm, and after him a long double line of his followers, rough fighting men, but now walking silently with black rags draped over their barbaric clothes.

The watchmen at the guardhouse over the causeway signalled with flag and horn back to the castle gatehouse and let down the bridge. The mournful procession passed through the gates. The Duke of Cornwall had come back to Tintagel.

They carried him into the great hall where Ygraine stood to receive him.

Uther approached her, handing his helm to his squire. He held out both hands. Dazed and wondering, she took them. The man's great blue eyes sought hers compellingly, and she felt the warmth of his hands penetrating her grief with reassurance and comfort, in spite of herself.

'I have brought him home with honour,' he said. 'He was a noble foe for many years. Indeed, I had come to think of him as a friend.'

She hardly heard his words, for there was something in his look, his voice, the touch of his hands, that disturbed her.

Gorlais had died at sunset, they said; yet, at midnight, she had led him up to her bower . . .

'I must see his face,' she said, and stepped to the head of the bier. She drew down the pall from the dead man's body.

Yes, this was Gorlais. The long, swarthy face, now waxen; the well-known features – and yet . . .

She looked from the dead Gorlais to Uther, bewildered. Backwards and forwards she looked between the two. There were no tears in her eyes, only strangeness.

Uther raised her right hand to his lips.

'Dear beloved lady,' he said, 'all my counsellors and wise men tell me that you and I should be wed.'

She stiffened and drew back a little.

'For reasons both good and bad,' he said. 'One good reason is that Cornwall and Loegres should be one, as we should be one. Another is that you need a protector. And for the bad reason – that I adore you, my lady.'

She turned her head to and fro between the dead and the living. 'So soon?' she said.

So it was that not much more than a month after the burial of Gorlais, there was a wedding in the castle, and Uther insisted that all should be done with all due pomp and ceremony. At the same time, Lot of Orkney, a tough, brown-bearded Northerner of strange speech, arrived after travelling all the way from his distant island kingdom to wed Morgause. She was smug, secret and chuckling.

'I shall have my wish,' she told her sisters.

'You will have sons, of course, by this Orkneyman,' said Vivian.

'I don't mean that. I mean our mother is pregnant and I shall have my baby brother.'

Vivian was astonished. 'How do you know? When did that happen?'

'You should know. That's why they hastened the wedding. You can be sure I shall not travel all that way to Orkney until the child is born. I've made up my mind on that. Perhaps I'll carry him off to Orkney with me.'

'Carry who off?' said Vivian.

'The son of Uther – or is it of Gorlais?' said Morgause, smiling wickedly.

It was the March equinox, and the storm hurled itself against Tintagel at the fall of night. The solid stone building shuddered, its timbers creaking. In the great hall there was no sound of jollity this supper-time. The fire alight in the hearth was sending up choking waves of smoke that blew this way and that, and the men-at-arms had taken their bread and ale and slunk into the corners away from the fire. Uther Pendragon had come down to them and told them that he would kill with his own hand any man who made a noise, for Ygraine was in travail, and it was going hard with her.

In the dark and draughty passages of the women's part of the castle, Vivian and Morgause met under the flickering light of a torch. Morgause was trembling, distraught.

'Oh Vivian, help me, help me. I'm frightened.'

'You – frightened?' This was incredible. Morgause was always so self-contained and placid. Moreover, Morgan was the one she always turned to, not Vivian.

'Yes, I'm afraid. Not for myself, for the baby. My brother, Vivian! Yes, I know quite well it must be a boy, and so do you. But it's Morgan I'm afraid of.'

She clutched Vivian's arm and Vivian could feel the coldness of her hand.

'Morgan's always saying he will be her adversary. She's walking around now, twisting a silken handkerchief in her hands. Oh Vivian, it's my brother, my brother – and I can't let her destroy him. There's no one I can trust but you.'

'Olwen La Nourrice is with our mother, isn't she?'

'Olwen is a witch, and the witches have to do as Morgan tells them, you know that. Presently Olwen will let her in, with her silken handkerchief.'

Even Vivian began to tremble with pent-up emotion. 'But what can I do, Morgause?'

'You can use your white magic. I can't, I never learned it. It took too much time and concentration.' She laughed uneasily. 'It's so much easier to hate and curse. But you, you can invoke the white powers.'

'I'll try.'

A stronger gust of wind in the darkness below gave a

sign that a door had been opened and closed. There was a step on the stair. It was Merlin.

Merlin! He came as an answer to Vivian's prayer – and yet, whenever she thought of Merlin now, it was with misgivings and a sinking heart. His actions had been so strange. He had seemed to condone what Morgause had done with the love potion, and he had brought that man who looked like her father into the castle. And yet, he was Merlin, and she stretched out her hands to him in the dark.

'Morgause, child,' he said over Vivian's head, 'will you run up to our laboratory and fetch me the flask of hart's-horn?'

As soon as Morgause was out of hearing, he drew Vivian into his arms.

'Vivian, you are the one I must trust now. And I must ask you to do some very strange things. Can you promise to do exactly what I tell you when the time comes?'

All misgivings were swept away by his warmth and power and certainty.

'Oh yes, indeed. Oh, I do trust you, Merlin. I'll do whatever you say.'

'Wait for me awhile, then,' and as Morgause returned with the flask, he went up the dark stairs to the Duchess's chamber.

It was about an hour afterwards that he came back to the two girls. His face was very grave.

'Vivian, I want you to come to your mother. No, not you, Morgause. Only Vivian.'

Vivian entered the birth-chamber. It was oppressive and close, and full of dim flashing lights. A fire burned in the great chimney, the flames and the smoke tossed about by the gale. Facing the fire, and taking up most of the space, was the large curtained bed. Olwen and two midwives moved uneasily in the shadows. Merlin, in his white robe, stood out amongst the darkness. Away at the back, in the darkest corner, sat Uther, crouched down with his hood pulled over his face. Between the two men was a cradle, and in it Vivian could just make out a swaddled form.

Merlin led her quickly and quietly inside the bed-curtains. By the bedside was a little table with a taper, a pen and inkhorn, and a sheet of parchment. Ygraine lay sunk in the bed, ashen-faced, hollow-eyed.

'Vivian, daughter,' she said, in a hoarse, faint voice. 'Come in closer. I want you to write. Vivian, I am dying.'

'Oh, no!' cried Vivian. 'Oh, Mother, no . . .' She turned desperately to Merlin. 'Merlin, it can't be . . .' But Merlin shook his head sorrowfully and laid his finger on his lips.

Dazed with shock, Vivian took up the pen, groped her way to a stool, and prepared to write.

'In the name of God, Amen,' said the faint voice. 'Write this, daughter, I haven't long. I, Ygraine, Duchess of Cornwall, swear this as I hope my soul may be saved. Now, write the year, the month, the day. Lady Day is it? Yes, I do swear this. My husband, the Duke Gorlais of Cornwall, was slain outside Castle Terrabil, on the twenty-fourth day of June last year, at the hour of sunset. I, not knowing this, at midnight that same night, welcomed a man who came to this castle, similar in every way to my husband. I took him to my bed. Then was begotten the son I have just borne, who has been baptized by the name of Arthur. Later I knew that the man who had come to me was Uther Pendragon, in the likeness of my husband. So I attest that this child is the lawful son of two fathers, and Uther Pendragon's heir . . .'

The faint voice faltered. She moved her hands feebly on the bedclothes, trying to pull off her signet ring. 'Seal it,' she whispered. Vivian helped to draw the ring from her finger, while Merlin heated wax over the taper, and pressed down the seal.

'Vivian . . . keep the writing . . .' The voice dwindled away for the last time.

Vivian fell forward upon the bed, weeping. When she looked up she saw, almost before her head had turned, from the corner of her eye, Uther pick up the baby from its cradle and hand it to Merlin. Now Merlin was speaking low and urgently to Vivian.

'Go and put on the thickest clothing you have, and meet me as quickly as possible at the entrance to the Great Cave. Go now, at once.'

She got shakily to her feet and went out, seeing as she went Olwen and the midwives drawing the sheet over her mother's face.

Only by leaning heavily on a staff and holding a lantern before her did she get down to the Great Cave. She knew it well, and had done from childhood. That tremendous arch of rock through which the sea would thunder at high tide. Even at low tide, when there was no more than a runnel of water, there would be a chuckling of pebbles, echoing against the roof, almost as a warning. And now, as she stood shrinking on the beach, it was as black as hell above her, and the wind howled as the tide came in.

She was suddenly aware of Merlin standing beside her, and she nearly collapsed with relief. He was holding something within his cloak.

'Vivian, my dear,' he said, speaking close to her ear to defy the storm, 'this is what you have to do.' Opening his cloak he let her see that he was holding a small, swaddled baby in his arms. 'Take him, my dear. Yes, you and no one else. With no mother, how could I have left him with Morgan, who would kill him, or Morgause, who would ruin him? You, Vivian, are now the Lady of the Lake, Nimuë. You are to keep him in a place where I shall send you, until the time comes. A boat is coming for you.'

'A boat?' She eyed the foaming waves with fear. There, drawing in close to the angle between the shore and the arch, was a coracle, just a circular bowl of stretched hides. A man was standing in it.

'Come, dear, climb in,' Merlin was urging. 'It's quite safe, much safer than it looks. Sit low, and clasp the baby tightly.'

She was about to step in when she heard shrill, screaming voices behind her. There, waving lanterns, came Morgan and Morgause.

'My brother! My little baby brother!' Morgause shrieked.. 'How dare you take him away. Bring him back to me!'

And Morgan growled in her deep voice, 'Give me that child. Vivian, you fool, give me that child. Merlin, I know you are my enemy, but so is he. I command you, bring him back to me.'

'Not so, ladies,' Merlin answered with a mocking bow.

'I do not think that it would be a good thing for my Arthur to be left with either of you. At least allow him to grow up.'

'Vivian!' Morgause shrilled across the sound of the storm. 'Vivian, you *traitor*! You're taking him away – *my* baby brother. How dare you! I curse you, Vivian, I *curse* you.' And she pointed her fingers at Vivian while her face screwed tight with abject rage.

'You fool, to think you can protect him from me!' shouted Morgan. 'You haven't the magic. Look now—'

Vivian felt herself buffeted by an onslaught of hatred from Morgause, but as she watched she saw Morgan draw on the power of the storm. Morgan was using her shapeshifting abilities to convert the wind and rain into a tangible being. In the darkness something greater than the dark began to swirl around, and rapidly it coalesced into a giant human form, rising to the very top of the cave, but totally black, with no features. Its arms began to reach down to Vivian.

'Run, Vivian, into the boat,' commanded Merlin. 'Let me deal with this.'

Merlin placed himself between Vivian and the black beast. Vivian at first felt rooted to the spot, but in that moment the baby uttered a small cry, and that was enough to prompt her into action. She hardly dared turn her back on the creature, which was even now folding down over Merlin, but she knew she did not have the strength to combat it. Not here, not now. She retreated to the shore, where the boatman helped her into the coracle.

She looked back but could no longer see Merlin, or her

sisters. There was only total blackness, but within that blackness a movement of something rushing towards her like a funnel of wind in the night.

And then a blast of foul, cold air struck her, threatening to knock her overboard. It swirled around her like a tornado, and she felt she might even be lifted out of the boat. She was totally helpless. Nothing she could do could combat that feeling of being totally overpowered. Then in that darkness she suddenly heard Merlin's voice. She did not understand a word he was saying. It was something ancient, something from the books that were banned. Here was a power as old as time, and it needed a spell from the dawn of creation to combat it.

Somewhere in the darkness that enveloped Vivian she could sense that there was a fierce struggle taking place. The primeval powers of order and chaos were deadlocked in their battle for the baby. She must, she *had* to do something to help Merlin. If the powers were so equally balanced, it might not need much of her own magic to make the difference. But she had never mastered elemental forces. Her powers were those of wood and stream, tree and flower . . . and *earth*! Of course . . .

She concentrated hard. It was difficult. There was too much going on around her to allow her to remember everything properly, and she must protect the baby at all costs, but she focused her mind, and deep down came the spell of the riven rocks. As it formed in her mind, so she channelled the power back to the shore. At that same moment a lightning strike illuminated the sky. Its power was almost instantly absorbed into the darkness ahead, but a little of that power came to Vivian and her spell formed. A barrier of rock rose out of the sea between the coracle and the cauldron of darkness. It shot skywards like an impenetrable cliff and around her the sea bubbled and churned.

Vivian clutched the baby, the boatman grabbed at his oar, and as the coracle was propelled away from the land, Vivian fancied she heard a cry from Merlin, but just what he said, she was not sure.

6. The Lady of the Lake

The first mad whirl of the coracle almost robbed Vivian of her senses. There was nothing but giddiness, darkness, and the crashing of the waves. Then, as the coracle came for a brief minute on to a straight course, she recovered her wits a little, but only to experience fear and helplessness. She had never been in a coracle before. She had expected that Merlin would be with them, but she had no idea whether he lived or not. There was nobody but the silent boatman and the baby, clutched in her arms.

She carefully shifted it into a more comfortable position in the crook of her left arm and wound the cloak firmly round herself and the child, as she had seen the peasant women do. She was not unused to small babies, having helped Morgause and the midwives around the castle. This one, clasped so close to her body, stirred deep feelings of tenderness in her. The poor little mite, too soft and vulnerable for any place less warm and safe than that from which it had come. Was this any way for a child to begin its life? Unless this child was destined for greatness. If so, then Vivian knew she would have to protect it, guard it, help it against a world of enemies.

She could see nothing in the impenetrable darkness about her; she could only feel the ribs of the coracle against which she was leaning. She found her girdle, a stout silken cord, and bound herself securely to a rib. And then the confusion fell on her again. A wind, like a hammer-blow, hit the coracle and spun it round once more, and the vast waves lifted it up and plunged it down. All was lost in chaos, without direction, without pause. Above all the wind shrieked on an unbearably high note, like a woman screaming. And below, the dark rumble of the storm threatened from the black abyss.

Vivian was grateful she was not prone to seasickness, though this did not stop the fear of her situation threatening to make her scream. The torment went on and on. The sea was becoming more turbulent. Ice-cold waves crashed over them. She hunched her body closer over the baby which, amazingly, slept through all this. Vivian wondered whether Merlin might have placed a sleeping spell upon it. She moved her cloak slightly for fear of stifling the child. Her mind was racing, the events of the night playing over and over again. Merlin returned to her thoughts, and again, for a moment, her trust faltered. What was this greater plan in which Merlin was involved? Just what had he done, and what part was she now playing?

Her thoughts moved away from Merlin as the coracle rushed up an even more mountainous wave and dropped like a stone on the other side. The shock wakened the child with a violent start. It began to whimper, then to wail, then to scream. She held it warmly, reassuringly, though she felt none of that herself. Almost without volition she caressed the child, soothed it, while all the time the chaos tossed them to and fro. But all in vain. The child was hungry, that was only too clear.

'Oh, my little darling,' she spoke to it as if to herself. 'What can I do for you? I can give you nothing.'

With surprising energy the tiny fists clawed at her, tearing at her clothes as if in a frenzy. She could not see, but felt the determined little morsel of life struggling, fighting her, and all the time screaming. It knew what it wanted.

In desperation she felt her way through her garments and put her nipple in the baby's mouth. It fastened on like a leech and sucked avidly. To Vivian's astonishment she felt, incredibly, unmistakably, the milk flowing in her breasts. The baby was suckling and being satisfied.

An uncanny, sick misgiving came over her, even in the mindless tumult of the storm. Milk! No virgin could give milk from her breast, save only Our Lady . . .

. . . and witches! The cold thought sickened her. Yes, witches, though some of them were virgins, could give suck. They gave suck to the creatures that were their familiars – hedgehogs, bats, toads, snakes – sometimes from extra teats that appeared on their shoulders, or necks or their arms. Some said it was not milk but blood that they gave to the creatures. Some said that they were not virgins, but the brides of Old Horny.

Vivian knew herself to be no witch, just as she knew herself to be a virgin. She had never taken the vows of a witch, though she had been allowed to watch some of their rites. Neither had she ever come into the presence of Old Horny. A frightful thought occurred to her – what if Merlin were Old Horny himself? What had Merlin done to her?

Yet the baby had no such misgivings. Sated, it closed its eyes, or so she judged in the dark, and sank back to sleep. Peering up from under the bowl-like edge of the coracle, it seemed to Vivian that the waves were abating a little, and the darkness passing. She could see the crouching shape of the boatman. More in need for some human reassurance than of anything else, she touched his shoulder. He shrugged off her touch as if it had been an insect and did not look up. The action, small though it was, made Vivian feel even more alone and anxious. She took comfort in the understanding that the waves had certainly abated and that daylight was growing. She lowered her mantle a little and looked down at the baby's face. It looked back at her with wide blue eyes, startlingly blue. Suddenly the baby was no longer 'it' but most certainly 'he'. She bent her head and kissed the little face.

The coracle had ceased its violent twisting and danced gently on the water. The sun was rising and the coracle was moving along a narrow inlet from the sea, between banks that grew higher, less bare, more wooded. The inlet turned and wound till the sea was out of sight and the water lay calm. They were now moving along a narrow twisting channel between dark pinewoods. As the first ray of the sun struck through the trees they came to a wide, calm loch. Mountains all round closed it in, and the forest ran down to the water's edge. In the middle of the loch was a small island. The shape of a building showed between the trees. The boatman, still without a word, steered towards the island. It had a marble landing stage. The boatman manoeuvred the coracle carefully alongside and moored. Vivian was so absorbed in watching his handling of this difficult operation that she did not look up until she was suddenly aware that there was a hand outstretched to help her out of the coracle. The hand was Merlin's.

'Merlin! Oh, thank the Gods you are safe!' This was her immediate outburst, and even though the unsure thoughts about Merlin's actions rushed fleetingly through her mind, she knew she was immensely relieved to see him.

'Come, my dear. Give me the baby first. Is he safe and well?'

He took the baby gently from her and handed him to a placid-faced peasant woman who was standing patiently behind him. Then, as Vivian, hardly able to keep on her feet, stood awkwardly balancing in the coracle, he took her boldly and bodily round the shoulders and knees and lifted her ashore. With his firm hold came a deep sense of security and reassurance. He carried her, just like a baby, through the trees, up long marble stairs and into the stone-built house saying, as he did so: 'Welcome, Lady of the Lake, into your own domain.'

There were so many questions to ask, but Vivian was so tired that no sooner had Merlin laid her on a couch than she drifted off to sleep. It was the servant-lady, Mae, who, while Vivian slept, removed her wet clothing, washed and dried her, and tucked her into bed, laying new clothes beside her. Vivian slept all day and all the next night. When she woke she felt fully revigorated, but still confused. Her first thoughts were of the child. She dressed and rushed into the next room, where she found Merlin sitting quietly in a high-backed black carved chair.

'Merlin, how is the child? Is he all right?'

'Good morning, Vivian. It is nice to see you up and about. Yes, the baby is fine.'

'He must be christened to protect him from evil.'

'He has been christened already. I christened him. His name is Arthur.'

She cried out in surprise. 'You christened him! But how . . . ?'

'Yes I, my dear. You should know that anyone can christen a child, or a grown man for that matter. Anyone, even if not a Christian himself. And Vivian, I know that there are those who say I am no Christian. There are some who would make me out to be the Devil's son. But those are people who do not know me. What do you think?'

Her eyes dwelt on his face, but she did not answer.

'Yes, I made myself his godfather, though we must presently have other godfathers, I well know from where.'

'I could be his godmother.'

'Not you, my dear. I have a reason why you should not, but I'll tell you that later. Look, there is much to talk about, but you must be hungry. Come, sit down, have some breakfast. You are safe here, on the Isle of the Lake. The lake is called Nimuë, and you are the Lady of the Lake.'

Merlin patted the chair next to him, and Vivian settled down by the table while Mae brought in a bowl of porridge for her and some bread, milk and fruit. Vivian was astonished at how hungry she was, until Merlin told her that she had slept for over twenty-four hours.

A little while later Vivian was sitting comfortably beside a large log fire built up in a great chimney-piece with iron firedogs. She was in a deep armchair, nestled into rugs and cushions, her feet on a thick sheepskin. Opposite her sat Merlin in his more austere black wood chair. By now Vivian had taken in more about the house itself. She was in the only large room, or hall, of the stone house. It was not large, as such houses go, but it was comfortable. A deep layer of fresh rushes covered the floor, with rugs of animal skins spread over them. Carved coffers were arrayed round the room, strange and faded tapestries, still beautiful, adorned the walls, showing scenes of hunting that flickered in the firelight. Close beside Vivian, in a cradle of plaited willow-twigs, the baby slept happily.

Mae, she had learned, was the wife of the doorkeeper. She was a cheerful, plump lass, simple, no doubt, but intelligent enough in all practical matters. She had a little girl a month old and her capacious breast had milk enough for two babies and to spare.

The house (Vivian started to call it her castle) stood alone on the island, raised up from the damp of the water by many steps. Beside the hall there was a large kitchen, some store-rooms, and a few simple bedchambers upstairs. Three men served as a garrison – the doorkeeper, the unspeaking boatman, and a rough-bearded giant of a man with a broadsword and axe who had two fearsome deerhounds and was ready to defend Vivian and the child against all comers and all powers – except perhaps magic.

'I was so sorry – the Powers Above know I was sorry – to put you to such a perilous journey. But Arthur's life was in danger; the most precious life in Britain, *for* Britain, in this age of the world.'

They turned together and looked at the child where he lay sleeping peacefully.

'He is born not only to be the leader and king, but the soul of his people, in his lifetime and long after. He had to be born of those two, of Ygraine and Uther. It was only by Morgan's working that Ygraine did not marry Uther in the first place . . .'

'Morgan's doing? But she wasn't born – she is the same age as me. How could Morgan . . . ?'

'Morgan is older than you suppose – just as I am older, and you, too, Lady of the Lake. Morgan is the deathless child of ancient evil and goes from body to body. She desires to rule this realm of Britain for her own dark purposes and so she sought to frustrate the destiny of Arthur, the son of the Pole Star, and she procured herself to be born, sister to you and Morgause, like a cuckoo's egg in a hedge-sparrow's nest.'

'I always felt she was no sister of mine. But what of Morgause?'

'Yes, Morgause is your sister, but being a weak and sensual creature, Morgan has easily dominated her.'

'She'll not dominate me.'

'Amen to that, I'll say, and you've already proved it by escaping from her magic at Tintagel. But she is very powerful. She would seek to kill this child and so set back Arthur's time on Earth for who knows how long? Long enough for her evil purposes to take root and make this country a land of devils. So I had to snatch him out of her reach and send him and you a long, long way away.'

'But how did you get here before me, and what happened after I left?'

'There are more ways to travel than by land or sea,' Merlin responded, enigmatically. 'Morgan's venom was aimed at you. Once you brought up that barrier of rock – for I imagine that was your work – her ire ceased and she and Morgause fled back to the castle. Her dark demon rapidly faded and I was able to escape by my own means. But Morgan will not stop. She has tried all kinds of ways to hinder Arthur's coming into the world. First by causing Ygraine to be married to Gorlais; then by entering Ygraine's nursery herself, hoping that then there could be no child of Ygraine and Uther. So, my dearest, I had to contrive – yes, it fell to me – that Arthur should yet be born of his destined parents. That is why I had to work all sorts of strange ways, even Morgause's love potion, to ensure that Arthur should have the blood of Uther, and yet be born without guilt or violence. Yet I did not know that Gorlais was to die; I could have waited but a few hours. But there – the wisest of us cannot know everything. Those few hours would have meant different stars, that I do know.'

'But Morgan did nothing to hinder your plan – she almost seemed to welcome it.'

'Morgan was willing enough that Arthur should be born, if it so be that she could kill him, for that would have meant a long wait until the stars came round again for the next birth of the spirit that is Arthur, and in that time she could have had her way.'

He fell silent, gazing into the fire.

'And is the child safe now?' she ventured.

'As safe as I can make him. I have put flowing water between him and Morgan and, as you know, running water is a bar to the power of most witches. He must remain here, with you, for a time, and then he must go to a man whom I have long had in mind – Ector, son of

Briareus, son of Constans. His brothers are Bors, Lioncel and . . . Torion.'

She winced as with sudden pain and crossed herself.

'Torion? I once knew him.'

'I know you did, my dear. You wrought no harm to him. Morgan used her arts on him; you were not to blame. Ector, his brother, is to be this child's foster-father, for I have great hopes of those three brothers. The boy will need them. But not for some years yet. Meantime, you must keep him here. Are you willing to do this for me, and for him? For as many years as may be needful?'

'Oh yes, of course, Merlin.'

'Then, as he has been baptized, he must be received by a priest. I know a hermit, and will bring him here by ways he will not know. For Vivian, my love, mark you this. His presence here must *not* be known. Not to anyone. Therefore, though I will put up strong magical protection, you must *not* use any magic. For Morgan, though not your spiritual sister, has a sympathy with you. She can vibrate to your note, and if you sound any note of magic, she will feel it and be drawn to you. So, no magic. You must trust me to put up all such spells as are needful.'

'I understand,' she said.

He drew close to her.

'One more thing. I shall bring the hermit here to receive Arthur and acknowledge his baptism, but this priest can also make a marriage. Vivian, will you be my wife?'

Without a moment's hesitation she turned into his arms.

'Oh yes, yes.'

He caressed her and rather solemnly kissed her forehead.

'My dear, you are so trusting. You so young, and I so old. Dare I lay all this burden upon you?'

'It is no burden,' she said, her eyes radiant.

7. Mischief Afoot

Merlin was always having to go away. Vivian took this as part of the order of things. Now, as the summer drew on, he left her again with his great gold ring on her finger. The boy Arthur was growing and thriving and Vivian was becoming used to her strange household.

'No magic,' once again he impressed on her. 'I have done all that is needful here. I shall not be away long.'

So, as she walked the garden by the edge of the lake and enjoyed its beauty, she was content. Until she noticed the birds. She had seated herself on the stone seat overlooking the marble steps, and Mae had placed little Arthur on her lap. There was a fluttering by her shoulder and a water wagtail brushed her cheek with its wing. Another wagtail flew down to her other shoulder. A whistle, as of some bird unknown, sounded from the willow trees, and the wagtails answered it, first one, then the other. Then a pair of magpies, smart in their black and white, flew down and paced to and fro on the grass at her feet. Their china-blue eyes went this way and that, turning their sharp gaze on the baby. Vivian felt disturbed.

'See those birds?' she said to Mae.

'Why, mistress, it's only that they love to see the baby,' Mae responded.

'May be, may be,' said Vivian as another whistle sounded from the trees, and the magpies answered it. 'Come, I think we'll go in. Take the baby.' And very deliberately, to avoid any suggestion of alarm or panic, she retired. The whistles followed her, and a robin answered them on the threshold.

It was too much for her. In spite of Merlin's warning, she set up her protection spells, circles and pentagrams, all of them specially guarded against Morgan. Only then could she sleep safely – as she thought.

The hermit was an old man, slow-moving, feeble. It took him some seconds to rise from his low seat, where he was meditating, and go to the door. On his doorstep was a lady, tall and dignified, wrapped in a long, black cloak, with a hood that covered most of her face.

'Bless me, Father,' she said, and genuflected. He blessed her, as he would any who came. She must be a pilgrim, he thought, though why any pilgrim would come to his lonely spot, he did not know.

'May I come in?' she asked. He hesitated.

'I have a very private matter to tell you,' she said, sighing as if she bore a sorrow.

'Then please come in, lady, come in. My place is poor.'

Indeed it was, nothing but a small stone cell lit only by a hole high up in the wall, furnished with a straw pallet and a wooden seat for meditation. There was a cross painted on the wall. The lady entered and, without asking, closed the door behind her.

'Have you no light here? I beg you, light a taper.'

She waited while he struck fire and kindled a rushlight. Then her manner changed, and she stood commanding him.

'Father Kyle,' she said, 'I want you to answer some questions.'

'Y-yes, my lady,' he stammered. From under her cowl her eyes glittered.

'Tell me, when did you last baptize a child?'

'When?' He fumbled through his memory. 'It was last Christmas – the daughter of Hubert the gamekeeper, over the hill . . .'

'No, no! Not as far back as that.' The lady made angry gestures with her hands hidden within her cloak. 'Lately, man, lately.'

'No, lady, I baptized none lately.'

'You lie!' Her anger flashed out at him. 'I know you lie. You baptized a child not a week ago.'

'No, lady, I swear . . .'

'Do not perjure yourself.'

'Indeed, I swore to seal my lips.'

'You've already part unsealed them, old fool. Now, tell me.'

'But madame, I did not baptize him. That had been done before.'

'Ah-ha, so there was a child, and a boy-child, too. Very well, now you can tell me whose child he was, and where he is.'

'Madame, I dare not. I gave my word not to.'

'But you've already broken your word.'

'I must not.'

'Do you feel this, old man?' She withdrew one white

finger from her dark cloak and pointed it at him. The old man shrieked in pain, racked with a fiery cramp.

'The Lord between us and all harm!' he prayed, and crossed himself, but the holy protection had been invoked too late.

'Have mercy, madame,' he gasped. 'I'll tell you.' He felt the cramp receding. 'The child was named Arthur.'

'I thought so. Who were his parents?'

'Truly, at first, I thought it must be the child of the couple who had also summoned me to wed them, but not so.'

The lady's face, rather more visible now since her hood had slipped back a little, frowned.

'To wed them? Who were they?'

'Madame, that is another thing I am forbidden to tell.'

'You've told so much already you might as well continue.' The hermit winced as a warning twinge of the cramp shot through his old bones. 'Who were they?'

'The man calls himself Merlin the Mage, and the woman was Vivian.'

The lady flung back her head and shouted with laughter, but there was no pleasantness in the sound. 'By the Kingdom of Hell, that's rich. What a jest. Old Merlin.' Her laughter subsided into a chuckle. 'One thing more, old man, what was the place where you both baptized and married?'

'Oh madame, I cannot . . .' Again his body twisted in pain. 'Believe me, madame. I was taken there hoodwinked. I could see nothing. I never knew. But I think I heard one speak the name of Lake Nimuë.'

'Ah, the Lake Nimuë; I can find where that is. Thank you, old man, you've told me all I want to know.'

She pulled her hood over her face again and moved to the door of the cell.

'Here's to cure your cramp,' and she flung down a handful of gold coins.

When she had gone the hermit fell on his knees before the painted cross and wept. Presently he arose and, gathering up the coins, threw them as far away from him as he could.

Orders were that Vivian would see no visitors. But Morgan strode past the doorkeeper and past Mae, saying, 'I'm her sister,' and was in Vivian's bedchamber before Vivian could hear her coming. All the magical protections Vivian knew could avail her nothing, for they were all tuned to the key of her foster-sister and fellow student of magic.

Morgan had thrown off her black cloak and hood and was radiant in a white dress adorned with gold, with fine gold sandals. Vivian felt a peasant beside her.

'Why, sister.' She advanced, smiling, and planted a kiss on Vivian's cheek. 'That is to say, Mistress Merlin!' Morgan laughed. 'So, you're the old man's darling. Give you joy, I'm sure. Do you oil his bald pate, and put his white beard into curling papers? Come now, do you enjoy it?'

Vivian shook herself free from Morgan's hands.

'Morgan, stop it. He's not bald and his beard isn't white. You know quite well—'

'Oh, keep your temper, darling. All that I know quite well is that you always were a fool about him. Oh—' and she turned towards the cradle which she had pretended not to notice before, '—and you haven't lost much time, have you, in producing a fine boy? How old, would one say, and married not more than a week?'

'Morgan, you know it isn't my child. You know that it's Mother's.'

'Is it so, indeed? Well, well, our little brother. An interesting child.' She made to pick up the baby, but Vivian interceded.

'Don't you touch him. Keep away.'

'Why, my dear sister, don't you trust me?'

'Not an inch; and you're no sister of mine.'

'So? I suppose your dear old husband told you that and, of course, you believe him. My dear Vivian, there is a strong enough bond between us. All your magic is linked with mine, and your silly protections helped me to find you. I thank you, I'm sure. So, now let me see my little brother.'

She tried again to get past Vivian and approach the cradle. The baby woke and began to cry loudly, screwing up his little face as if he were in pain.

'Morgan, don't you dare!' Vivian snatched up the rosary that hung always above the child's cradle, and thrust the crucifix before Morgan's face.

'Oh all right, then!' said Morgan, retreating. 'Since I'm not welcome, goodbye, dear – but you'll find it hard to hold a crucifix over him all the time. We'll meet again.'

She swept out of the little room, quietly, quickly and self-possessed, leaving Vivian to clasp the child in her arms and try and hush his terrified crying.

A dark night, a new moon, cloudy, without even starlight. Vivian could not sleep, but lay staring at the dark.

Her little room was not unlike the one she had shared

with Morgan and Morgause at the farm in Roseland. The stone 'castle' on the island was little more than a farmhouse, adequately protected by the lake, and therefore built comfortably with casement windows to the upstairs chambers. Very like the farmhouse, to which Vivian's memories regressed. They had all been so comfortable there, and happy. They used to climb in and out of the window there, especially Morgan . . .

Morgan, always Morgan. No matter how she tried to stop, her thoughts kept returning to Morgan. It had been a week since Morgan had visited. Just today Vivian had returned to the farmhouse after a walk around the island to find a great bunch of wild flowers on the table, close by little Arthur's crib. Late summer flowers, foxgloves, white convolvulus, honeysuckle – but it was not the season for them. They gave off a fresh country scent, yet was it fresh? It was rather over-sweet, sickly, ominous . . .

Mae came in. 'Why, mistress, you're soon back.'

'Soon back? I've been out for two hours.'

'But it's not ten minutes since you came in with these flowers.'

'I never brought in these flowers. There's none like that in bloom yet and, anyway, I never came in ten minutes ago.'

'Begging your pardon, my lady, but you did.'

'It was not I, Mae! Who was it, eh, who?'

'Oh my lady, I would have sworn it was you. You even spoke to me . . . oh, mistress . . .'

Vivian snatched up the flowers and flung them out of the window. She bent over the baby with anxiety. He was sleeping, heavily and not healthily. She took him up and carried him down through the hall and into the open air, shaking, slapping, even pinching him to wake him. He woke at last, dull and peevish. She trembled over him, and fed him carefully till he seemed normal again.

Morgan! So, the battle had begun. And Morgan would not stop there. In any case, that would have been too peaceful and painless a death to satisfy Morgan's cruelty. She would try something much worse next time.

Vivian moved Arthur's cradle to the far side of the bed, next to the wall. Nothing could reach the child but over Vivian's body. Vivian sprinkled holy water round the crib and suspended a crucifix above it. But would this really be enough to keep Morgan out?

As if in answer Morgan suddenly appeared at the window. She stood balancing on the window-sill and, kicking back her robe, swung her long legs over into the room. Vivian gave a little scream and moved to shield the baby. By the dim, glimmering light in the room she could see Morgan, luminous in her white dress.

Morgan spoke in a soft, rustling whisper, like a snake moving over dry leaves. 'Good evening, sister.'

'Keep away,' said Vivian. 'Do not touch the child. In the name of the Highest Power Above, do not touch the child.'

'As you please. I shall do him no harm. It's more likely that *you* may harm him.'

'What do you mean?'

In answer, Morgan's long pale fingers pointed at her, and Vivian felt a change coming over her. Many a time all three sisters, for practice or sport, had changed their shapes into all sorts of things, not only human shapes, but animals, plants, even stones, but Merlin had forbidden them ever to use that power on others. Never did he allow them to change the shape of any other being, not even to turn a wasp into a bee. But here was Morgan turning the power upon her. Vivian was changing. She felt the hairiness of an animal. Her tongue went out and licked a long canine snout. A dog? Then she looked down at herself. A wolf! A long, lean grey she-wolf.

'Good evening, loveliest of she-wolves,' said Morgan's mocking voice. 'Are you hungry? But of course you are.'

Vivian could feel one half of her mind sliding towards that of the animal: the wolf's simple concepts of fear, rage, hunger. A dim impression stuck in her mind of a litter of young wolves, left behind in some cave, small furry bodies and foxy faces. She felt the flow of milk within her, but feebly, not in the woman's breasts but in the thin hanging dugs of the animal. Hungry, thirsty, the little ones needing milk. And close beside her was a small, hairless animal, fresh and fat.

'You're very thirsty,' the soft voice went on. 'And see, what big teeth you have. Use them. Kill it, suck its sweet, red blood. It's none of yours – your young ones are whimpering in the cave for milk.'

A part of Vivian's mind was horrified and retained its hold on humanity. *I'm not a wolf; I'm a woman. I'm Vivian. This is a baby, a human baby. I'm Vivian. I'm* . . . Her human name seemed to elude her. Now she could not remember it. She tried to pray, but the words meant nothing. And Morgan's voice went on hypnotically.

'You're thirsty, so thirsty. Go on – kill, *kill*.'

In the darkness Vivian was aware of the long, sinewy, hairy body that was now hers, stretched out on the bed – the furry throat, the rough paws, the spreading pads, the jaws, the teeth. The window was open. She could jump through it and be gone – and then? Wander howling round the house until she found . . . ? With all her strength she resisted. She was a woman, not a wolf, she was . . . Vivian! With an effort she regained her name.

'Oh, you're putting up a fight, my silly little she-wolf. Very well, try this.'

Suddenly Vivian's shape changed again. She was a tiger. She felt the soft, luxurious fur. She stretched out her limbs before her and saw the huge, sharp claws flash from the velvet sheaths. She raised herself on the bed and caught sight of her face in a mirror on the wall in the pale light that seemed to glow from Morgan's dress. She knew her own eyes were green, but the eyes that stared at her now were as green as emeralds, lucent with green fire. Again her human mind began to fade and the quick rage of the animal exploded within her. The craving hunger, the furry cub somewhere in her den, needing milk, hungry, hungry, thirsty. And here, a small tender creature almost beneath her vast spreading paw, fragrant of fresh meat, juicy and delicious.

Morgan was softly hissing, a sound that worked on the tiger's nerves, exasperating it. A remnant of human consciousness fought in her, now rapidly sinking into a horrified spectator of the frightfulness to come. The tiger crouched over the baby, sniffing, slavering. One fragment of human consciousness plucked it back. Morgan hissed again. The tiger turned to face Morgan, and as its swelling rage broke, sprang straight at her.

Morgan vanished. The tiger's claws landed on empty air. She could hear Morgan's mocking voice. 'Not me, beautiful tigress. There's no flesh and blood in me, but there's flesh and blood just there, beside you.'

The animal's baffled rage boiled up in her into a red tide. There was no holding it now. It had to have blood.

In desperation Vivian caught her own forelimb between her teeth and closed her jaws on it. She felt the bones crunch and the blood gush out. The shock of the atrocious pain broke the spell. There she was in her own shape, bleeding, shivering, with her arm crushed above the wrist. But Morgan was gone, and the baby was safe. A white light seemed to radiate from the baby. A sound behind her made her turn, and there was Merlin.

'I felt you were in danger,' he said. 'She's gone. Let me see your arm.'

He held her arm and the bleeding stopped; she lay sobbing against him. He began to stroke the injured arm, singing strange words over it. Vivian felt the pain recede and a deep sleep crept over her. When she woke Merlin was lying beside her and her arm bore no more than a circle of small scars. Arthur was awake and laughing.

PART III

The King Hereafter

1. A Sword for Arthur

Merlin came rowing the boat over the loch on a calm sunny morning. He rowed in the way the southerners do, standing up and facing forward, with the oars crossed before him, so he could see the lake island of Nimuë coming into sight, and the gleam of the white walls of the little castle.

It was an older Merlin by some fifteen years. If, as he had seemed when he first came to Tintagel, he was in his early forties, he must be nearing sixty now, but a vigorous handsome sixty. Not bald, for all Morgan's jeers, his thick, black hair was now well streaked with silver and glittered in the sunlight; his beard, still black, was bushy and spade-shaped, his hair falling over his neck to meet it smoothly. His teeth flashed sound and white, and his dark blue eyes were as bright as ever. Yet there was a look of stress about him, as if he were never free from thoughts of anxiety.

The approach to the island showed many changes since the morning when he had first brought Vivian there with the baby Arthur. Trees had been cleared away and others planted. Flower beds, bright with colour, bordered the marble stairway. All along the water's edge, roses overflowed and shed sweet petals on the water. The rose briars made a thick screen and hid the strong fence that ran along the water-line, not so much to keep intruders out as to keep childish feet from slipping into the lake. A strong gate closed the landing place, but it was standing open now.

As he brought the boat alongside a lovely little girl, nine years old, ran down to meet him. Her black curls were like his own, but her eyes were green.

'Father, Father,' she cried in her clear, shrill voice. 'Oh Mother – Father's home.'

Behind her, at the top of the steps, were Mae, now grown fat and matronly, and Mari, Mae's daughter, a sturdy lass of fifteen. Behind them stood Vivian, the sunlight touching her red hair, slim and light-footed as ever. The little dark-haired girl was more light-footed still. She bounded up the stairs and back down again to Merlin before her mother could so much as look below and smile as Merlin approached. The little girl was dragging him up by the arm, and babbling to him.

'Now you're back, we'll have fireworks, and stories, and magic. Did you see Arthur? How is he?'

'Certainly I saw Arthur,' he said, chuckling at her. 'Considering I spent the last six months teaching him.'

'Teaching him what? Magic?'

'Well, no, not *much* magic. No more than he will need. You see, he isn't going to be a magic man.'

'Not a magic man? What will he be?'

'Something very different; perhaps something better.'

'A knight? Is he to be knighted, then?'

'No, not a knight, or not yet. He couldn't be until he's eighteen, you know. His foster-brother Kay is to be made a knight at Christmas. No, Arthur's to be something else—'

'I know! I know!' She jumped up and down in excitement. 'A king!'

At that moment they reached the top of the steps and were caught in Vivian's embrace. Merlin was drawn into the welcome of his little household.

Blaisine was his only child. He gathered her into one arm and Vivian into the other. Blaisine – he had christened her so after his old master, Blaise, the great magician of Brittany. From her earliest days she had shown herself full of strange powers. How could she fail to be gifted, with such parents as she had? She had everything in her small way – the Clear-Sight, the instinctive control of the weather, the remarkable sympathy with animals, the healing hands. If Vivian had a headache, or Merlin himself, it was Blaisine's cool little hands that soothed it away. She was a quick learner, picking up a great deal of magical technique without really trying. Merlin, in spite of all misgivings, and his desire that she should be a happy, normal child, could not refuse to teach her.

She was not really a solitary child, although she had not yet set foot outside her little island. There was Mae's Mari, and there had been Arthur, the adored big brother. But since he turned ten, when Blaisine was four, Arthur had gone away to live with Sir Ector, and Sir Ector's two brothers and his kind wife, and though he often returned on visits, the time between the meetings seemed very long to Blaisine. Mari, though good-natured, could not share Blaisine's thoughts, and more and more she drew in upon herself. Vivian watched her with understanding.

Blaisine chattered on to Merlin as they went up towards the house. 'Father, look, there's the place where the Little People were last night. They're here most nights when the moon's full. Do you know, Mae can't see them at all, nor can Mari. Aren't they stupid? Arthur could always see them. Can he still?'

'I daresay he can, my poppet,' Merlin replied, 'but I don't think they come around much where he is now. There're too many people. But there are other things he'll be able to see, in time.'

'Is he coming back to us soon?'

'Not yet. I'm afraid he's going to be very busy. But we'll all go up to see him at Christmas, when Kay is to be knighted.'

Blaisine clapped her hands and capered. 'Oh lovely, lovely. But I wish Arthur was to be made a knight as well.'

'Wait and see, Blaisine. Arthur's turn will come. We need a sword for Arthur.'

'A sword? Oh, that's easy. There are plenty here hanging on the walls. There's the one he used to play with.'

'That's too small for him now. You'll have to see how big he's grown. No, we want a special sword for him, a very special sword.'

By now they had reached the house, and Merlin set Blaisine down. She scampered off to fetch her father's slippers.

*

After supper Blaisine recognized preparations that she was familiar with.

'Oh, Father, you're going to make magic tonight. Can I come in too?'

He put his hand caressingly on her head.

'I'm afraid not, sweetheart. Your mother and I are going to make magic, but it's not very nice magic. Not for you.'

'How do you mean – not very nice? You don't mean *black*?'

'No, no, but it's rather frightening.'

Blaisine made big wide eyes, as she always did when her father spoke of spooks and phantoms. Her experience of magic and nature had made her bold and bright. Little frightened her, although she still jumped if someone crept up behind her unawares and pounced on her. She accepted her father's explanation, though she remained curious.

'Come, Blaisine,' said Vivian. 'Time for bed. Your father and I are going to be busy tonight.' They both hugged the little girl and kissed her goodnight, and she trotted off to see Mae.

Vivian and Merlin now prepared for the adventure ahead. Merlin had not had much opportunity to explain to Vivian what was expected. She had helped Merlin prepare his satchel of phials and charms. He now led her out of the study and along the corridor towards the steps to the cellars. By the side of a door was a small alcove.

'Take a candle,' he said in a voice deep and solemn, 'and follow me.'

'Where are we going?' The candle in her hand shook a little.

'Down – a long way down.' And he led her down a stone stairway that she had never descended before.

Although the little castle was very compact, beneath it were cellars and vaults of unknown depth extending down through the mount on which the house was built and into the rock of the island, possibly deeper. In the fifteen years that Vivian had lived on the island there were some of these into which she had never ventured. Of course there were wine-cellars and wash-houses and store-rooms, all of which Mae took care of, and Vivian never went there. But further down, she knew, were places where Mae did not go, nor anybody else. Their entrance was enough for Vivian. She did not like their look or smell or sound or feel. But here it was that he was inexorably leading her.

He halted for a moment and set down his candle.

'We are going into a very dangerous place,' he said.

'Is it Morgan again, after all these years?'

'No, not Morgan. For the moment the stars are against her, which is why we must work fast, before the stars pass. I must have a sword for Arthur, and the keeper of the sword will not give it up easily.'

'Who is he?'

'You have heard people speak of Old Nick?'

'Of course – that is what some call the Prince of Darkness,' and she crossed herself.

'And yet they are mistaken. Some that have heard that name bestow it on the Evil One, almost in jest. The one I refer to is Old Nekr, or Neckar, as the northerners call him. Those of the northernmost isles call him Shony, or Jonas. It is he that lives in the utter depths, in darkness and slime, where everything goes that drowns and decays.

He is not Neptune, nor Poseidon, whom the Greeks knew as the ruler of the waters, Jove's brother, that shakes the earth. Neckar, Old Shony, is darker and more deadly. He should be subject to Poseidon, but he is a disobedient subject who has remained cut off from his brethren for too long. Down here in the slippery residue of drowned worlds Shony can evade all rule. His daughters are the Nixies, beautiful but deceitful. Shony himself has something of Proteus, for he changes and slips away and eludes those who would bind him. It is he we must seek now.'

'Why must we?' she whispered, as if afraid to disturb the silence and rouse the denizens of the deep.

'Because it is to him that all the lost treasures go that men cast into the sea, or lose in shipwreck. He hoards them. And his treasure of all treasures is the sword I must have for Arthur – the sword Caliburn.'

Picking up his candle again he led on, down into the darkness and clamminess.

'We are below the water now,' he whispered. The walls each side were damp and slimy, the roof dripped above them. Black shreds of some dark growth hung down like wet rags. The smell of decay was overpowering. On they went into the darkness.

They halted in front of a door, blank and black. Vivian saw Merlin's hand wave, tracing figures, and heard him muttering strange words. Then he thrust firmly against the door, and it opened.

Beyond was a chamber, no larger than a closet, and all its walls were inlaid with shells. They caught the light of the candles and gleamed back against the darkness – a mosaic of shells, disposed in geometric forms. Directly in front, as the door was opened, was a central panel which bore a crude figure, depicted with larger and more luminous shells. It was the figure of a man with a fish's tail. The clumsily drawn tail curved round below the figure. Its human arms spread out to right and left. The face was round and doll-like, but a doll's face that was both stupid and malignant. A grinning mouth showed a row of saw-like teeth.

Vivian remembered the mermen that she had seen with her sisters all those years ago. Old Shony must be their lord, or the father of their race. She also remembered how she had helped one of them that Morgause had injured.

Merlin placed his candle in a sconce on one side of the figure and beckoned Vivian to do the same on the other side. He motioned for her to kneel in front of the figure and bow her head. Then Merlin began to chant in a low and resonant note.

'Shony, Shony, Shony. Neckar, dweller of the utmost depths; Deva Jonas, lord of the innermost dark, I call upon you.'

He paused, but all was silent. He repeated his incantation. Still there was silence, but Vivian had a sense that something was listening, something that was not far away.

Merlin tried a third time.

'Shony, master of the eternal deep. In the name of Poseidon the Mighty, I call upon you to answer me.'

From the black wall before them, as if from the figurine, came a voice, rusty, grating, deep and ancient.

'I am here. Who calls me, and what would you with me?'

'It is I, Merlin.'

'Merlin. It is many wrecks since last we spoke. But you are not alone.'

Merlin turned to Vivian. 'Tell him who you are.'

'It is I, Vivian, the Lady of the Lake.'

There was a long silence, and Vivian began to fear that Shony had taken objection to her presence. But then the voice returned.

'Vivane,' it pronounced the name in a long, slow, whisper, with an emphasis Vivian had never heard before. 'How long it has been, my spritely Nimuë. I welcome your return.'

Merlin touched Vivian's hand and squeezed it as if to say things were working well.

'Shony,' Merlin continued, 'I require a gift from you.'

'A gift. What gift?'

'The sword Caliburn.'

There was a hiss as of indrawn breath.

'What I have I hold, Merlin.'

'That is why it must be a gift, Shony.'

'What will you give me in return?' The voice took on a note of cunning.

'For that you must wait and see. Your gift could save mankind.'

'What is that to me?'

'Without the sword an evil will return to the land which will not stop in the destruction of all that is good and holy. It will devour everything in its path, including you.'

'Then I should keep the sword and use it for my own protection.'

'It will not work for you, Old Neckar. It will work only in the hand of him who is Destined.'

'I see little reason to help mankind. Mankind has never helped me.'

Vivian squeezed Merlin's hand and motioned to be allowed to speak. Merlin was curious, but consented.

'Shony, it is I, Vivian. I once saved one of your folk, a young merman who broke his arm on the seashore near my father's castle.'

'I know, and I thank you. But your help only balanced the debt incurred by your sisters who injured Kiwiatti in the first place. I owe no debt.'

Merlin now interceded. 'Then I command you in the name of . . .'

The word he spoke could not be heard by Vivian's ears, it was too thunderous and resonant, five, six or seven syllables echoing on and on, shaking the earth above.

'I must obey your command,' the voice responded. It sounded softer and more meek now, but with a definite tone of resentment. 'Caliburn is far away at the bottom of the Great Ocean.'

'Then send your slaves to fetch it. Now!'

Vivian was aware that the presence had gone. She stood, easing her cramped muscles. 'How long will he be?'

'Who can say?' Merlin responded. 'I do not believe the sword is that far away. It is one of Shony's most treasured possessions and he would keep it near him. We must just wait and see.'

There was silence for a while, before Merlin commented upon Vivian's early episode with the merman. 'I had not known of that. You continue to be full of surprises to me, and always such wonder. Your chance encounter, twenty-five years ago, might be our salvation now.'

Vivian mused on the many chance encounters in her life, such as that with Torion, and wondered how many paths led away from them for good or for ill. One might be a creature of Destiny, but one could never predict it.

Suddenly she became aware of the return of the presence.

'Merlin, I have the sword.'

'Then give it to me.'

'No, not to you. I shall give it to the friend of my people, to the Lady of the Lake herself. But she must come and take it. She must row her boat to the head of the loch and I myself shall give it to her.'

Vivian listened with a sinking heart.

'I shall come with her,' Merlin countered.

'You will not. If you are in the boat then you both shall drown and I shall keep the sword. She must come alone. I will not harm her.'

'Nor shall you, Old Neckar, or by the most Ancient Name I will send the fires below to destroy your secret kingdom.'

'I have said all that I shall say,' returned the voice. 'Nimuë must come alone, and must come now, before dawn.' And the voice was suddenly still.

'Depart in peace,' said Merlin, and he stepped backwards out of the small chamber and closed the door. He held the candle above Vivian's head.

'Dare you, my dear? I know you will, but the Gods forgive me for sending you into this.'

They went quietly and quickly up the stone stairs and

passages to the outer doorway. It was still night, but the faint moonlight seemed dazzling after the darkness below. Merlin led the way down to the water's edge. The roses, exuberant over the edge of the loch, gave a sweet scent as they passed. Vivian breathed it deeply and gratefully, after the dead smells of that underground chamber. It was a still and overcast summer night, the moon's light diffused behind the clouds, showing the paleness of the gleaming water between the dark trees.

Vivian fetched the little light boat they used for crossing the lake. Merlin had brought a cockerel to serve as a sacrifice, which he bound and placed in the boat. Before Vivian stepped into it, Merlin held her close to him and they kissed. 'My dearest lady, go with care,' and he lifted from around his neck his pendant. Vivian had never seen him without this charm, his greatest protection. Without it, Merlin was at his most vulnerable. Vivian hesitated, but Merlin thrust it over her neck and muttered an incantation. 'Go,' he commanded, without further ado, and stepped back from her.

She seated herself in the boat, facing astern and, with a few strokes, she sent the boat moving swiftly away from the steps. She looked over her shoulder to check the way she was going, but after one look she kept her eyes fixed on the tall white form of Merlin as he receded from her. He stood motionless on the landing stage like a pillar of light in the darkness, and the vision of him gave her the strength and resolve that she needed.

The loch opened into the sea, and all its seaward extent was tidal. The water rose and fell once a day, making a fresh interchange between fresh and salt water; but at the head of the loch was a stagnant creek where all the floating rubbish and refuse drifted and stayed, sinking into the black ooze. Dark, sour plants grew there, and yew trees and black alders overhung the bank. By day the air was full of pestilent midges. At night, stealthy creatures moved between the dark bank and the waters. No one went there, but that was where Vivian rowed her boat, softly in the darkness.

Once she felt the boat scraping on the mud and the mess of broken branches, Vivian shipped her oars. She picked up the black cockerel which Merlin had placed in the boat and lifted the bird by its feet, hanging its head over the side of the boat. From her waist band she withdrew the sharp sacrificial knife which Merlin had given her and, with one swift single movement, she sliced off the cockerel's head. The bird struggled and fluttered horribly in its death reflex and the blood spattered into the lake. She held it for a moment and then dropped it into the bloodstained water.

'Shony,' she cried, her heart beating.

All was silent, and then the water began to ripple. In the dim light he came up out of the water: first a smooth hump, like a thick black bubble, then it became his head, then his shoulders – greenish black, streaming wet, with long slimy hair oozing down over the featureless face, but through it a gleam of cruel eyes and sharp teeth. There was the foulest stench of fermenting vapours that Vivian had ever encountered and she found it hard to breathe.

Gasping, and attempting to stand upright in the rocking boat, she called out, trying to keep her voice from shaking.

'Shony, as commanded by Merlin, give to me the sword Caliburn.'

The apparition spoke from under its streaming hair.

'Are you Nimuë, the Lady of the Lake?'

'I am Nimuë.'

'Then come and get it!'

The creature gave a harsh, barking laugh and held out, with black, shrivelled hands, a long sheath-like shape. Still seated in the boat, she turned half round, keeping a grip on the thwart with her left hand, and with her right reached out and seized the shape. Undoubtedly it was a scabbard, which she held by the point end. Shony, laughing again, pulled back and wrenched out the sword, leaving her with the empty scabbard.

'Here it is. Swim for it if you want it!' He flung the sword in a shining arc far over his head and out into the lake. With a final bubbling laugh the baleful presence was gone, though the waters boiled for some moments more.

After a minute's utter dismay and loss Vivian grasped the scabbard in both hands. An ancient thing it was, slippery with the mud of the sea bottom, but discernible as a piece of leatherwork overlaid with bronze. More by touch than by sight she made out the runes on it and pronounced the words written there, aloud over the water. Then, pointing the open end of the scabbard out over the water she summoned the sword.

'Caliburn, blade of Destiny. Arthur's time has come. I, Nimuë, Lady of the Lake, call you, in the NAME which Merlin has invoked.'

The words echoed off the surface of the water.

In the middle water, reflecting the rays of the moon, the sword Caliburn gradually rose above the waves. As if brandished by an arm its hilt circled three times, and then the sword skimmed over the surface as if drawn by a lodestone, straight to the boat's side. Vivian reached down, still afraid of feeling Shony's slimy touch, and drew the sword up, quickly placing it back in the scabbard. Then, all in one movement, not staying for one instant, she picked up the oars and struck out for the island. All the time, as she rowed, her eyes were fixed on the dark creek where Shony had risen, but nothing more showed itself. When she turned her head to see her way, there was Merlin, like a beacon, standing stiff and upright on the steps. His arms received her safely, and he held her tightly for a long while. Then he took back his pendant, muttering another incantation. Only then did he take the sword from her. His hand traced a pentagram against the black water of the distant shore, banishing any claim Shony held over the sword.

'By the grace of the Mighty One,' he said, at last, 'Arthur has a sword.'

In the firelit hall of the little castle they examined the sword. Merlin laid it on the table, having first carefully laid down a cloth, lest any fragments of the scabbard should fall. Both sword and scabbard were blackened, corroded and crumbling. With great care Merlin drew the sword from the scabbard and laid it by its side. The blade appeared to be of some dark brown metal; the hilt was of a strangely beautiful shape, cross-formed but curving; the quillets, or side-pieces, were outlined in garnets and agates, which even in its decayed state caught the light; the pommel was one round, perfect white crystal, now clouded grey like the moon.

Now that the blade was withdrawn the scabbard looked ready to fall to pieces, for it was made of many small metal parts set upon leather, now shrivelled and cracking, like so much rotten wood. Merlin lit a lamp and looked closely at the craftwork.

'This is very old,' he said. 'Very, very old. It was made in the days when all weapons were made of bronze, and yet it is not all of bronze. It is a subtle mixture of all the seven metals: gold, silver, iron, quicksilver, tin, copper and lead, made by an art long ago lost to man. I knew the man who made it, in another life. By strange and cunning ways, he made it. Some of the metals he melted and mingled; others he interwove into the inscription on the blade. By the interchanging of the natures of the seven metals, a powerful magic was put upon the sword. Though it comes from the days of bronze, yet there is a power upon it that could cut through steel. That is why it is called Caliburn – "Cut Steel" in one of the old languages. I know a man who can restore it, blade, hilt and scabbard. Tomorrow I will go in search of him.'

'But Shony?' Vivian said, still trembling.

'Shony will not harm you now. You have paid him his due, and he will not ask for more. Never fear Shony.'

'All the same, I'll keep away from the head of the loch. And can we seal up that place underground?'

'We shall, my dear. But have no fear. From now on, Arthur's star is rising.'

2. Arthur the King

A fine bright summer morning and, along the coast road northward, towards Berwick-on-Tweed, rode the young King, Arthur, as handsome as the day. He rode at the head of his band of knights, all his dear and personal friends: Sir Ector first, who had long been his guardian, and Sir Ector's brothers, Sir Bors and Sir Lioncel; Sir Ector's son, Kay, Arthur's foster-brother, older than he and now his seneschal; also Sir Griflet, Sir Ulphius and Sir Brastias, all bound together by oath to serve Arthur and his land of Britain. They were a small band, but numbers were constantly being added.

The knights wore armour that distinguished them from all others; armour which Arthur, with Merlin's help, had designed from the patterns of the old hauberks and helms, leg-pieces and arm-pieces that the family had inherited from the Romans. But they had adapted and altered the designs and made them something better and more suited to the needs of the time. The helmets had been fitted with bristling crests of wild boar's hair and tall plumes of wool, dyed scarlet.

Their horses were also remarkable: tall black horses of

the kind the Romans had brought to Britain, long-legged, smooth-necked, small-headed. Horse and rider together made a gigantic figure. No one else on the island had such horses, such great black devils, with their rolling eyes and spreading red nostrils. These were for the knights alone. The squires, pages and other followers rode the stocky British ponies from the moors.

At the back of the troop rode Merlin, also on a black horse, conspicuous in his white robes. Dear old Merlin, was how Arthur thought of him – father, counsellor and friend, who guided him through the perilous road of kingship that had been his for three years now, ever since he had pulled that sword from the stone. A rather older Merlin now, to be sure, heavier in build, stouter, his hair long and mostly white, but still streaked here and there with black and grey.

As they rode, Arthur cast his mind back over the astonishing life he had led. First there had been the life in the little castle on the lake where Merlin was and yet was not his father, and Vivian was and yet was not his mother. Vivian's gentle influence made everything beautiful. And there he had sisters. There was Mari, Mae's little girl, just of an age with himself, and there was Blaisine, Vivian's baby, whose arrival he dimly remembered. Although he called Blaisine his sister, she was told to call him uncle, whilst Vivian, whom he regarded as his mother, was apparently his sister. It was all rather confusing, but nothing to worry about. They were all rather sweet and comforting, and it had been an idyllic childhood.

Then there was a change. When Arthur was about ten, very much against his will, and with tears on all sides, he was taken away and put in the house of Sir Ector, with Sir Ector's brothers and his big son Kay, and his gentle, comforting wife Lady Anna. He had been very unhappy at first, but Lady Anna had been kind to him and Vivian and Merlin often came to visit him. It was a strange old house, away in the comfortable vales of Devon, built mostly of timbers and clay, but partly using the stone walls of a far older house. Those stone walls were painted, and part of the floors were made of squares of coloured stone, laid in patterns and pictures. Lady Anna wore dresses just like those shown in the wall pictures, as she said that her mother had, and her mother's mother, and so on back to the times when the pictures were painted. The family kept the old Roman ways and were Christians, and kept a priest in the household who said Mass every Sunday in their little chapel.

This had too, after all, been a good life, once he became used to it. There was the excitement of hunting, learning to ride, first on the little British ponies and then mastering the great black war-horses. There was shooting with the bow, fighting with the sword, axe and mace, and all the manly arts. But when he was fourteen years old, the Lady Anna died and then, by imperceptible degrees, everything changed. With no women there at all, not even serving-maids or a housekeeper, the atmosphere became grimly masculine. Hardihood, hardship, hardness – that was the order now. Hard bed, cold room, bare table – food in abundance, but coarse and carelessly cooked. Plenty of ale – often, too much. Not a hint of softness, grace or pleasantry. The flower garden was rooted up, to be replaced by beds of onions. Vivian and Blaisine still visited Arthur, and exclaimed with dismay at the bareness of it all, but poor Sir Ector, without his wife, could scarce be blamed. When they left, Arthur missed them more than ever.

Then had come that strange day when he had drawn the sword from the stone and found himself King of Britain. He should have known what was coming, of course, what Merlin was preparing for him. Yet, how should he know? Kay and he made a joke of it, a private game of 'If I were king . . .'

'If I were king,' said Kay, 'I'd have everything magnificent. I'd have a big black Roman horse of my own, bigger than Father's, and I'd get the old smith to make me the finest suit of armour ever, one that *nothing* could penetrate. And I'd have a Damascus sword; I'd get an army together to go to the Holy Land and turn the Turks out once and for all, and I'd come home with a Turk's head on my spear and cartloads of gold and silver taken from the Infidels, and a princess to be my wife, or maybe two princesses, or three or four, like the Turks. What about you? What would you do, if you were king?'

'I think if I were king,' said Arthur, 'I'd like to have the armour and black horse and the Damascus sword, but not to go to the Holy Land, or not yet. I'd want to put things right here, first. I'd set poor Jehan free from his bondage and send him back to his wife, and I'd stop old Sir Breuse up there on the hill from making his peasants work for him for nothing. I'd let Tamsin at the mill marry young Hal, instead of letting her father sell her to old Grimbold. I'd stop the lord hanging poor poachers. Oh, all sorts of things.'

Kay laughed. 'Is that all you'd do? Oh my dear Arthur, you've got no imagination.'

'Imagination? Of course I have. I'd like to imagine the poorest peasant in my land having a chicken in the pot for his dinner every Sunday. I'd like to make my kingdom so that a beautiful lady covered with gold and jewels could walk alone through the length and breadth of the land and fear no harm.'

'Ha!' said Kay. 'That won't be seen this side of Kingdom Come.'

But was it imagination that took hold of him that day in London? They had all been excited, for Kay was to enter his first tourney. There had always been gatherings for games at the great festivals of the Church – contests in wrestling and boxing and singlestick, and baiting of bears and bulls, cock fighting and dog fighting – but lately more polished sports had come in, some said from France – combat on horseback and on foot, carefully and formally regulated by law and custom, and courteously dedicated to the ladies. Sir Ector and his friends were great upholders of these arts, and with lords from further away, they had organized some of these big formal gatherings. There were lords and barons who looked on these events with suspicion – such an assemblage seemed to them like a bid for power, and they preferred to keep their power in their own hands. For, since Uther Pendragon had died, there was no king in Britain. Each lord was supreme in his own lands, and made his own laws, good or bad. Some were very bad indeed. Such lords had no wish for any gathering of power and refused to come to the jousting. In some cases they held sports of their own, of a kind closer to slaughter than showmanship.

But Merlin planned the greatest joust ever, in London, in the precincts of the great church. St Paul's they called it, a tall structure on a hill by the river, where some believed Saint Paul himself had once preached. Others said that it was a Saint Pol or Paulinus, but it was all so long ago, and nobody really knew. But there was the church, and the wide space below it and, as the parties came in sight, that crisp December day, there were many coloured pavilions all round, and timber houses with bright draperies hanging from the windows, flags flying and trumpets blowing. All Sir Ector's family was there to see Kay's performance. He was to be made a knight before the tourney. Merlin had brought the Lady Nimuë of the Lake, whom Arthur still called Vivian, and her pretty dark-haired Blaisine, and even Mae and Mari, all in their best clothes, to do honour to Master Kay. Arthur had been all eyes and ears, not regarding himself at all, but quite taken up with the spectacle and novelty.

And then the extraordinary thing happened. Kay had left his sword behind, and Arthur, running back to fetch it, found himself locked out of his lodging. Nearby was a pavilion and this beautiful sword stuck in the stone. Thinking nothing but that he must borrow it for Kay, and would replace it later, Arthur had drawn it out. At that moment something seemed to come over him, so that he was no longer himself. The moment passed and he was once again a frightened and anxious boy. They made him put the sword in again and draw it back out, a dozen times. He could not understand what had happened – what he had done. Then they were all kneeling to him, dear old Sir Ector and his brothers, with Sir Ulphius and Sir Brastias and all the rest, and the Archbishop was presenting him to the people, and the men-at-arms were shouting, and the Lady Vivian was weeping as though her heart would break, and then smiling and laughing and kissing him. It was all a remarkable commotion.

After that there had been troubles and worries, and moments of wonder, too. Becoming a king was hard work, even with Sir Ector and the others to organize and fight and worry for him, and with Merlin directing everything from the background. He was crowned at Whitsun, but even then not all of the lords would accept him. Sir Ulphius and Sir Brastias had some fighting to do, but they would not let Arthur fight, not till a good two years later. But he was allowed to keep the sword. Merlin gave him the scabbard, too, and told him mysteriously that the scabbard was even more magical than the sword, and that he must never lose it. He kept the sword and scabbard belted to his side, and he was never seen without them. Every time he took the sword from the scabbard, the strange feeling came over him, growing as he grew, the feeling that he was more than himself, that power entered into him, that something lifted him out of his mortal being. Sometimes there were things he saw or heard, but he told these to nobody, not even to Merlin.

Following Merlin's advice, Arthur went on a Royal Progress round his dominions, or those dominions he claimed in right of his father, Uther Pendragon. These were hard to define, as maps were few and inadequate. Mostly the rivers formed boundaries. Throughout the land, lords and barons had set themselves up in castles, some of which were no better than robbers' strongholds. It was these that he set out to visit, with his ever-growing band of knights. At each one he would approach with his flag of peace and invite the lord of the castle either to accept him as king and pledge fidelity, or to fight in the way he chose – preferably by single combat, or by a mêlée of no more than six to a side. Nobody wanted the tedium and unpleasantness of a siege. Mostly the lords submitted cheerfully and received Arthur as their king – they were sick of lawlessness. Feasting and cordial hospitality were the order of the day. But when they had to fight, they fought. For the most part, Arthur's men were successful, since they were better armed and trained. But now and then they had to admit defeat and withdraw. In those cases Merlin kept a list of the castles to visit again. Where Arthur was victorious, many of the barons, or their sons, joined themselves to Arthur's band. He made them knights, with a solemn ceremony, and a vow that included not only fidelity to Arthur, but certain duties, such as to use no violence or fraud against any man, to use courtesy in manners, to protect the Holy Church, and to respect and defend all ladies, gentlewomen and womenfolk of every degree, young or old, for the love of our Blessed Lady.

And so they rode north. Arthur, on Merlin's counsel, intended to go as far as the town of Berwick, but not to set foot in Scotland. The King of Scotland, Angus (but called Anguish by some), had agreed to meet him at Berwick. There the Scottish King would cross the river under a flag of peace and make an alliance with Arthur, with a great feast. Merlin counselled that they should advance no further north.

'But there are islands further to the north,' said Arthur. 'Orkney and Shetland.'

'We are not to go there,' said Merlin. 'The Queen of Orkney is your sister, and you are not to go there.'

'What, another sister?' said Arthur, laughing. 'But why should I not go visit my sister?'

'You are not to go there,' said Merlin, frowning and abrupt, and would say no more.

3. The Wonderful Ship

So he rode northwards, in all the handsomeness of his eighteen years. Not only his tall, well-made frame, his almost perfect features, deep-set blue eyes, chestnut hair, smoothly rolling down his neck, but the vitality, the exuberance of young life, unspoilt and untried, the lightly tanned skin ('like prime pastry', someone had said), the velvety golden bloom on cheek and chin, all as fresh as if he were the first man, new-created. And still untried in love. His life on these journeys had, for the most part, been severely masculine, like his home life with Sir Ector. The castles they entered were often devoid of women. Occasionally noble ladies would welcome them, and made much of the handsome young King, but he was afraid of these grand ladies. On the other hand, in many of the castles there were plenty of willing wenches, but Arthur hesitated, fastidious. He did not want his first sexual adventure to be a sordid one. In any case, he had enough to occupy him without bothering about women – yet.

An echoing call was passed along the ranks from behind, and the cavalcade halted. Merlin rode up.

'My lord King,' he said, 'a word with you.' For so he

now addressed Arthur in public, though in private he was still 'Arthur-boy'. They drew in to the side of the road, in a clatter of hooves.

'Arthur,' said Merlin, 'you'll have to go on alone for a while. Those two knights, Sir Colum and Sir Keno, that were wounded in the last skirmish are in a bad way. Both have fever from their wounds. Unless I stay behind with them overnight, and do what I know I can do for them, I fear they'll die. You must go on, for you have to meet King Angus at Berwick tomorrow morning and, unless you are there on time, it will be taken as an affront. I'll have tents pitched here for myself and my patients, and you and the rest must go on. Be sure you reach Berwick by sunset, and make your camp by the seashore there. I'll follow as soon as I can.'

'Of course,' Arthur replied. 'You must do what you can for these poor chaps. I shall be all right.'

'God send you will be,' said Merlin.

So all that afternoon they journeyed on, and in the fine summer evening they encamped where the Tweed runs out eastwards to the sea, and across the Tweed was Scotland. The evening was serene; the northern summer sunshine lingering on over a sea like blue silk. Even the seabirds were quiet. Presently the sun, westering behind the mountains, slowly descended and flooded the sea towards the east with strange, rich colours. Arthur walked along the sea's edge, away from the camp. Behind him he could hear the stirring and clanking of men and horses, softly muffled by the distance. Then, lit by the western afterglow, he saw a ship approaching.

At first it was a tiny thing, like a jewel, something that caught the light and reflected it, flashing crimson as from many bright glass windows. Then, nearer, he could see the sails like the wings of butterflies, and here and there the rigging catching the light, like silver wires. Now, nearer yet, he could see an exquisite ship, gliding in unimaginable beauty. Her colour was emerald green, but touched with crimson and white and gold. All her shape was eloquent of speed and grace and loveliness. At that distance Arthur could see no mariners aboard her; maybe the distance was too great. But as she came ever closer, he could still see no one aboard. He knew nothing of ships and supposed, if he thought at all, that her crew were hidden somewhere. At the stern of the ship was a rich pavilion, hung with gold and crimson, its curtains closed. Many banners and pennons fluttered above the masts, but he saw no device he could recognize.

Some of the other knights had seen the ship now and came down to the beach to look and marvel. It was surely some great lord's ship of state, they said, but nobody could venture to guess whose. There was a little landing stage on the beach, and presently they saw a boat put out from the ship and approach it. One serving-man rowed the boat, and its passenger was a grave, elderly man in a long robe, who spoke courteous words of greeting to Sir Ector as he came down to the shore.

'I am sent to meet the most noble and mighty young King Arthur,' he said. 'My lady bids him come aboard and receive her welcome.'

Sir Ector hesitated, but Arthur stepped forward, forestalling any attempt to speak for him.

'And who is your lady?' he asked.

'My lady is the Queen of Hy-Brasil, the Isles of the Sunset in the furthest west. To meet the noble King

Arthur we have sailed from the Western to the Eastern sea, right around the northernmost Cape of Wrath, and have come hither to the coasts of the East. My lady is by name Madame Elaniane, the most renowned and beautiful. In hope that you, my lord Arthur and King, will one day visit her kingdom, she bids you now visit her little ship on these waters and sup with her this night.'

'Willingly,' said Arthur, without once looking back to Sir Ector or anyone else for advice. Merlin—? Yes, but Merlin was not there. Surely Merlin would not forbid him a real adventure, and surely courtesy commanded it.

'My lord King,' Sir Ector approached him, 'someone should go with you.'

'Your pardon, noble lords,' the ambassador said, 'this poor cockleshell of a boat will carry but one. But have no fear – your noble King will be safe with me.'

Sir Ector was frowning and shaking his head, but Arthur could not take his eyes off the lovely ship. 'I'll go,' he said, and without another word stepped aboard the boat and was carried quickly away as the dusk began to fall and the sunset colours fade from the sky.

The boat soon reached the side of the ship, where many coloured lanterns had begun to shine. Arthur was helped up a ladder to the deck and, without a moment to look around, he was led into the pavilion at the ship's stern. Here he stood amazed.

The pavilion was covered underfoot with carpets, soft and thick, that deadened all footfalls. Rich curtains closed it in and it was softly lit by one finely wrought lamp of many-coloured glass. There were deep chairs of a kind he had never seen before, full of cushions, and there were cushions scattered about the carpeted floor as well. Amidst all this he came face to face with the most beautiful woman he had ever seen.

Her dress was of a lovely clear blue, like the sea, and of a material so fine and thin, gleaming and flowing, that though it fell to her feet in an incredible wealth of folds, yet it was gathered so neatly round her waist that it seemed to clip close to the alluring shape of her body. The low-cut bodice outlined perfectly her small, shapely breasts. His hands, as he gazed, twitched with a sudden longing to caress them. And her face was too beautiful to gaze at for long, yet his eyes came continually back to it. Pale ivory, yet flushed with faint pink, like a rose, the eyes blue as forget-me-nots, the mouth as sweet as a child's. Her hair was loose on her shoulders, pure yellow gold, all a maze of shining curls. Arthur looked at her and looked away. He was overcome with her beauty and found himself all in confusion. He turned back to the entrance in panic for the old ambassador, but he had gone. Arthur was alone with this lady.

She took a step towards him, smiling, and clasped both his hands in hers.

'Welcome to my little ship, Arthur the King. I have long wished to meet you.' Her voice was soft and melodious. She turned to a little table and filled two glass goblets from a flagon. 'Let us drink to friendship between our kingdoms – Britain and Hy-Brasil.'

He drank and at once felt calmer, more relaxed. The wine was sweet and bright, as clear and cool as spring water. The lady continued talking and all of Arthur's fear faded away. After so much hardship, how wonderful it was to lie back in a soft chair, sip wine, let the perfume of roses that breathed from the lady sweep over him, her golden hair bewilder him and her blue eyes hold his own fixed as with a spell . . .

Darkness had just fallen when Merlin started up from the bedside of his two patients with a sudden urgent sense of misgiving. For some while his mind had been troubled; a feeling of threat clouded his thoughts, though he dismissed it as his anxiety for the wounded knights. Yet now they were both out of danger, the feeling of uneasiness and foreboding did not cease, but grew stronger, till it became unbearable.

'You must take charge now,' he said to his assistants. 'The men are out of danger, and will do well if you follow my instructions to the letter. I must go. I fear the King needs me.'

With a thunder of hooves, he swept into the camp at Berwick. Watch-fires and torches were burning, but there were more lights than usual after an encampment of this kind had settled for the night. The camp was restless and apprehensive. Ector and Bors were pacing to and fro on the moonlit seashore. Merlin vaulted from his horse, throwing the reins to a squire, and strode towards them.

'Where's the King?' he asked at once.

'Why, honoured Merlin,' said Ector, 'he's gone out to the ship to visit the Queen.'

'The Queen? What Queen?' Merlin almost shouted.

'The Queen of Hy-Brasil. She sent a boat to fetch him.'

Merlin gasped and flung up his arms. 'Oh God, the Queen of Hy-Brasil! There is no such thing. My good Ector, couldn't you tell? There is no Queen of Hy-Brasil.'

'Wh-who then, honoured Merlin?' stammered Ector.

'The Queen of Orkney. Fool that I was to leave him. How long ago did this happen?'

'Almost sunset. He went aboard her ship.'

'And where is the ship now?'

'Look, out there.' Ector pointed across the bay. There was nothing but darkness. 'By Our Lady, it's gone!'

'Glamour and illusion all!' cried Merlin. 'I must go to him and warn him . . .' With those words he sank to the ground in a swoon. He lay straight and rigid, his face like one in a deep sleep. As they looked, a strange thing happened. The end of his white headcloth, lifted by the breeze, flapped forward over his face. Then, as if a stronger wind lifted it, the white linen seemed to struggle and something white detached itself, like a clumsy bird, thrashing its wings to take flight. A white barn-owl sprang up and sent itself with strong, silent wing strokes towards the sea.

In that same instant another shape interposed – a great fish-eagle, black in body and wings, with gleaming white breast, neck and head. It launched itself towards the white owl. The owl circled and dodged, but the eagle was always between it and the sea. They clashed together, both shrieking, and struggled in the high moonlight over the sea. Then both crashed to earth. The spectators retreated from the shore as the combatants fell. As they touched the ground their shapes changed. They were two bears now, one black and one white, locked together, each scrambling with long claws to disembowel the other. Most horribly, they changed again: two slimy, snake-legged monsters of the sea, each towering unnaturally on the land, towers of writhing, heaped tentacles. Then the whole camp was shaken with shrill winds. The monsters were gone and, in their place, two whirlpools which rushed out over the sea, two waterspouts, the stream of the one white, the other green. The green waterspout was travelling out over the bay, but the white one, spinning like a top, came round between it and the open sea and clasped it, so that the white and green columns of water twisted like a rope and spun together. The terrified but entranced watchers, hardly able to stand against the tempestuous winds, saw, at the top of the whirling column, two colossal heads of barely human form. None could hear more than the moan of their whirling, still less distinguish words, but the two antagonists talked together in their strange, private world.

Do you remember, Merlin, we played this game once before, when we were both younger. She *looked out of the window, as white as any milk, and* he *looked into the window . . .*

Cease mocking me.

I'm not mocking now. That was a game. This is in earnest. My dear sister has her wish, I'm not letting you frustrate her.

I will frustrate both her and you.

You cannot. She'll have her 'baby brother' and possess him at last.

Only to beget Arthur's bane.

You cannot stop the workings of Destiny. You might turn the tide of events if he were not willing – but he is so very willing.

The shape that was Merlin groaned deeply and blazed upwards into a pillar of fire that clapped like a thunderbolt. The other became fire also. Higher and ever more vehement the conflagration grew. The men in the camp, which now was brightly and terribly illuminated, herded their terrified horses out of the way of the fire. The blazing shapes seemed to stream over the hills around, the solid earth shook and cracked, and thunder broke upon the roar of the fire.

Then silence. All was gone. All was dark and still, no light but the moon, and there was a little seabird, a tern, neat black and white, flitting across the face of the moon, and chittering *Too late now.* Merlin, lying as he had fallen on the ground, opened his eyes, lifted his head, rose to his feet and stood leaning on his staff, barely able to stand.

Across the bay the day was breaking. A small boat came quietly to the shore. A cloaked figure carried an inert body to the landing stage and, almost contemptuously, flung it down. Then the cloaked bearer and boat were suddenly gone, and there remained only Arthur, dazed and shaken, to confront Merlin, tall and silent. All could see, in the growing light, that Merlin's hair, from which the headcloth had fallen, was now white all over.

Merlin placed his arm around Arthur's shoulder and led him aside from the hearing of the others. Under a dark yew tree Merlin halted and turned Arthur round to face him.

'Well?' Arthur confronted him, sullen and defiant. 'What have I done, then? No more than many men have done before. I'm human, am I not, Merlin? I'm a man, am I not?'

'What have you done? Oh, Arthur-boy, my lord King, little do you know.' Merlin's voice was tremulous, as

Arthur had never known it before. 'You have begotten your own bane.'

Foreboding and fear-clouded, Arthur's eyes sought Merlin's.

'How so?'

'Arthur-boy, that lady was not the Queen of Hy-Brasil. She was the Queen of Orkney, your sister.'

'My *sister*! Holy God—'

Arthur sank on his knees with his hands over his face.

'Your sister. And on her you have begotten the child that is to be your bane, cutting short your reign, frustrating your work, bringing ruin to your kingdom. Oh, Arthur, the field of Camlann rises before me.'

'I had no idea,' Arthur said, fear, anger and bewilderment all evident in his voice. 'How could I know? Surely it was all glamour?'

'Indeed it was, all glamour – Morgause, Queen of Orkney, aided by Morgan, who is also now called her sister, your enemy and mine.'

'Could you not have prevented it?'

'Arthur-boy, all this night I have agonized in a deadly battle of high magic, to get to you and warn you. Morgan and I battled like cloud giants, and – I am weary, and she defeated me. She held me back till it was too late. But I could almost have defeated her, almost, I think, if you had not been willing. You consented to the glamour.'

Arthur dropped his head. 'Yes, I consented . . . I'll do penance, take my punishment, anything you say. Must I give up being king?'

'Give up being king? God forbid! No, stand up, boy. You must go on and consolidate your kingdom and fight for it, rule it. Arthur, that will be quite penance enough for you. Destiny is there to be fought. Come now, come to your senses. Let us go back to the camp. By the Powers, I need my breakfast.'

Arthur, rather more himself, looked at Merlin now, as he leaned heavily on his staff.

'Why, Merlin, your hair's quite white. So's your beard. I hadn't noticed it, before. How long has it been so?'

'Since tonight,' said Merlin. 'Maybe it is a record of the next chapter of Fate.'

And as they walked back to the camp Arthur noticed that Merlin looked older, as if the full weight of his years, and more, had suddenly come upon him all at once.

4. The Treachery of Morgan

So the years passed and Arthur came into his kingdom. The boy who had drawn the sword from the stone, the baby that had been carried in the coracle from Tintagel, was now the King of all Britain, and his kingdom was flourishing. At least for a while there was peace. The marauding Saxons dared not raid the coasts, and the churches and convents could do their work without fear. Arthur's knights, clothed in metal armour more efficient than the Romans', and mounted on their tall black horses, rode throughout the land imposing law and putting down brigandry. Arthur's court was the centre of honour and chivalry. With his queen, Guinevere, had come as a gift the great Round Table where his chosen band of knights seated themselves ceremonially. There were twice twelve knights, with the King, Queen and Merlin. Each had a place and a name painted upon the Table, two for each of the magical signs that only Merlin understood. No one else might be present, and there they worked a solemn and holy ritual. It was from thence that a power for good spread throughout the land, though only Merlin and Arthur knew what unremitting effort it cost to keep it so.

During those years Arthur had made some contact with his strange kinsfolk. Of his father's side, the house of Uther Pendragon, many had accepted him and were among his staunch supporters, though not all. On his mother's side, there were his three half-sisters. Vivian was always lovely and loving, though her continuing youthful looks earned her a doubtful reputation at Arthur's court. One of the chief talents that all three sisters had made their own was that of shaping and shape-changing; so Vivian, when in private and relaxed at home, would look what she was, a comely matron of forty. Yet, when she had to make a public appearance, she liked to exert her art and appear hardly more than twenty. It caused many of those at court, especially the ladies, to murmur, 'Look at old Merlin, doting on that young girl. His wife? Ridiculous!'

Her sister, Morgause, now secure as Queen of Orkney and the mother of a fine brood of sons, took less trouble. She was grown fat and overblown, and Arthur could hardly believe that she had been that Queen of Hy-Brasil, whose perfect rose-petal beauty had so beguiled him. Beside the four hefty sons of King Lot – Gareth, Gawain, Gaheris and Agravaine – she lately brought along one more, young Mordred, now rising seven, truculent and spoilt, for whom she was always asking special favours, which she knew Arthur could not refuse. In all the satisfaction of Arthur's achievements, the presence of Mordred was a shadow, a worry, a threat. And Merlin would look at the boy and shake his head. Merlin could see too far.

As for Morgan, she flashed in and out of the court, inscrutable, proud, menacing. She had taken as her husband Urien, lord of Rheged, a beautiful land of lakes far to the north of Britain, a strong and powerful man, but one who was gullible in Morgan's eyes. She had used him only to increase her power at court and amongst the northern lords. She was the mother of several children, but each looked so different that it was hard to believe that they all had the same father. Only Owain, with his dark hair, beetling brow and full-barrelled chest, was the image of his father. Talk had reached the court one time that Morgan had tired of Urien and had sought to kill him, but he had been saved by Owain who had been warned of Morgan's intentions by one of her handmaidens. Thereafter Morgan seldom visited her northern lands, and none were ever really sure where she had made her home. She came and went as she pleased at Arthur's court, incredibly beautiful, often most charming, but people were glad to see her go. Most glad of all was Guinevere, the lovely young Queen, who felt obscurely the power that radiated from Morgan, and dreaded it. Yet she made no objection when Morgan brought the young Lancelot to court and quietly placed his beauty before her eyes.

Whenever Morgan was at court Vivian became extra cautious. She knew that Morgan was constantly scheming, but over the last few years her plans had become more diffuse. Gone were any sudden attempts on Arthur's life. He was too well protected, not just by his band of knights, but also by Caliburn and its scabbard. Morgan sowed seeds of evil whenever she could and awaited their fruition. Although both Vivian and Merlin could perceive some awful fate, they could not determine how the weave of Morgan's tapestry of time led towards

Arthur's destiny. It was evident that Mordred and Lancelot were part of the scheme, but as yet their part remained to be played.

There was an instance when Vivian was able to perceive one of Morgan's games and intercede. It was one of the rare occasions when Morgan took a short-term opportunity to weaken Arthur's defences. Among the many knights at King Arthur's court was Sir Accolon of Gaul. He was a tall, strong knight, with long, dark hair, and was a powerful athlete, capable of outrunning most of Arthur's knights save the ever-fleet Sir Dodinel, who could run faster than a hind. There were rumours about the court that Morgan had taken Accolon as one of her lovers, but as Accolon was so intensely loyal to Arthur, Vivian had not considered this of any special concern. Morgan dallied with the affections of many knights, always for her own delight, never for theirs. After they had served their purpose she would beguile them in such a way that they would never remember that she had rejected them, but lived in the continuing belief that they alone had her special affection.

One day Arthur was out hunting with Accolon in the lands far to the east of Camelot. They had had a good day's sport, but were too far from home to return before nightfall so they went in search of a nearby hunting lodge situated within a wood. Both were in good spirits and exchanged stories and jokes as they wended their way through the gathering gloom.

'Accolon, had I realized you were such good company I would have gone hunting with you before,' said the King to his companion.

'And had I known you were such a good hunter, my

lord, I would have brought my own game with me,' Accolon responded, nodding at the weight of provender laid over Arthur's dray-horse, compared to the little which Accolon had killed.

Arthur laughed. 'Never mind, Accolon. Tomorrow it shall be your turn. Come, we must find this lodge, so that this meat can be prepared and cured and despatched to Camelot.'

They continued their way in pleasant silence for a half-mile or more when Accolon noticed a light flickering in the distance. He warned Arthur and the two peered ahead through the trees.

'It must be the lodge,' said Arthur, though he could not explain why both he and Accolon felt wary. They approached with caution. Gradually the trees made way for a large clearing where, beside the track, stood a small but most stately building. Accolon remarked that it looked like a castle in miniature. The building was perhaps twenty feet high and thirty square, but it boasted turrets and spires and battlements, all to scale. There was even a small drawbridge and portcullis. The bridge was down, across a narrow dyke, and the gates open, though the doorway was too small for Arthur and Accolon to ride through on their horses. Arthur went to dismount but Accolon gave caution.

As they watched they became aware of soft music drifting from the castle and lights moving past the windows and through the castle. In a while a procession of ladies, seven in all, clad in white, each carrying a candle, and each singing in soft, low tones, came through the gateway and across the small bridge, and arranged themselves in a crescent-shape across the front of the castle. Arthur could not distinguish one lady from another, they all looked alike. Their long dark hair flowed down over their white gowns. Their gowns were embroidered with gold and fur, and were covered in small sequins which reflected the candlelight in all colours of the rainbow.

The three ladies to the left and right knelt on the ground but the lady in the centre stepped forward.

'Welcome, my lord, King Arthur,' she said.

'You know me,' responded Arthur. 'Yet, how could you expect me?'

The lady did not answer directly.

'All are welcome at the Castle of Caer Ouzel, but none more welcome than the lord, our king. Pray enter and take rest.'

'Is this wise, my lord?' cautioned Accolon. 'These may be witches.'

'You may be right, Accolon, but how can we be sure? I wish Merlin was with us.'

The lady sensed their caution.

'Have no fear, my lord. This is a haven of rest. No harm shall come to you here, you have my word as a Virgin of Peace.'

Arthur had heard of the Virgins of Peace, an order of nuns who had established a convent at Glastonbury. Surely he would be safe in their hands, and he knew a way of checking.

'Who is the head of your order?' he asked.

'Our lady Arianhrod. She awaits within.'

Arthur had met Arianhrod several years before when he granted the nuns land at Glastonbury.

'It is safe,' Arthur whispered to Accolon. 'I know Arianhrod, and she is to be trusted.'

Accolon visibly relaxed. He and Arthur dismounted and led their horses towards the gateway. As they passed through, the darkness fell away. The courtyard within was a blaze of light as if the sun rose from the centre of the castle. Their eyes took some moments to become accustomed to the glare. Almost as if in response the light softened. Arthur was aware that several of the ladies had led their horses away. Ahead of him, in the centre of the courtyard, was a fountain which sprayed water as if it were light itself. It sparkled and glowed. As he approached it he became aware of its scent. An aroma of pure wine and honey filled his senses.

'He who drinks from the fountain of Caer Ouzel shall never die.'

The voice came from Arthur's left side, but he was so captivated with the fountain of light that it was some while before he turned his head. There stood Arianhrod, just as she had seemed years ago. Ageless, tall, handsome rather than beautiful, but above all matronly and caring. Arthur had no doubts that this was the real Arianhrod. He knew he would be safe in her hands.

Both he and Accolon were thirsty after their long ride, and the lure of the water made them feel thirstier still. Beside the fountain were several small cups on chains.

'Please, my lord King, and Sir Knight. Quench your thirst. It will replenish your strength and vitality.'

Arthur hesitated only momentarily. The heady aroma of the water, the sparkling light and the hypnotic voice of Arianhrod, along with the singing of the maidens, calmed and soothed him. He felt safe and relaxed. Both he and Accolon took a cup each, filled it from the fountain, and after one sip to slake their thirst and cool their throats, they downed the cup in one gulp. The water was like liquid fire. They could feel it coursing through their body and into their veins. A surge of power flowed through them and when Arthur and Accolon looked at each other their eyes were ablaze.

'I feel so strong and young again,' said Arthur, 'I could hunt a hundred deer.'

'And I could run a hundred miles,' said Accolon, 'and then a hundred more.'

They reached again for the cups, but Arianhrod stayed their hands.

'Not too much at once, my lord King; it is a powerful brew. Later. Come. Rooms have been prepared for you, where you may bathe and refresh yourselves.'

Arthur followed Arianhrod, unaware that behind him Accolon had started to buckle at the knees and collapse by the side of the fountain. Arthur's head began to spin, and the white glare of the fountain and the castle walls began to dazzle him until he could see nothing around him. Then came darkness and peace.

Accolon became aware of the sound of running water, and of a strong breeze, but his head ached and he was unable to open his eyes. After a few moments his head began to clear and he forced his eyelids apart. He could not believe what he saw. He was on a ledge near the top of a sheer cliff over which poured a waterfall which crashed on to the rocks and the sea a hundred feet below.

Had he but rolled a few feet to one side, his body would have plummeted to a certain death. Accolon found himself gripping the edge of the ledge, his heart pounding. He looked above him. The top of the cliff was no more than twelve feet above his head, but the rock face was sheer with no hand- or foot-holds, and one slip would be fatal.

Accolon wondered where he was. Ahead of him stretched the sea, disappearing into a blur of mist and horizon. He could see no sun or sky and had no idea whether it was morning or afternoon. His body felt cramped, as if he had lain there for a long time, but he was not cold, and did not feel damp, even though the waterfall crashed past him not ten feet away. He concluded that he could not have lain there long, and that maybe his body ached because of whatever had happened to him to cause him to be there. As he felt about him he was aware that all his clothes were intact, but that his sword and sword-belt were missing. His dirk, however, was still tucked on the inside of his left boot. Whoever had dumped him here had not searched him thoroughly. Perhaps the idea had been to kill him and throw him over the cliff, but chance caused him to land on the ledge.

Whilst Accolon was taking in the situation, and wondering whether he would have to climb down if he could not climb up, he became aware of a sound above his head. He flattened his back against the cliff and looked up. A face, square, craggy and rather ugly, was peering down at him.

'Is it Sir Accolon I address?' the face spoke.

'Who's asking?'

'One who might help,' replied the face.

'Who are you?' Accolon persisted. In answer, a knotted rope was thrown over the cliff, the end landing close to Accolon, but just far enough to be out of reach.

'You can of course stay there until you rot, if you so wish,' said the face, taunting Accolon by swinging the rope to and fro, always just inches from his grasp.

Accolon was always ready to tempt fate. With no word of warning he leapt off the ledge to the side and caught the rope. He had chanced that whoever was seeking to help him had already secured the rope to something strong, and this proved to be true. With his athletic grace, Accolon was up the rope and over the cliff face before his rescuer knew what was happening.

Accolon held tight to the end of the rope to use as a weapon if need be, and moved away from the cliff. Facing him was a small man, not three feet high, stocky and solid, dressed all over in black and with a thick tabard that made him look almost square.

'Well done, Sir Knight,' said the dwarf. 'You are every inch as agile as your reputation.'

'And you are every inch as ugly,' Accolon retorted, annoyed at his treatment, though also thankful that the dwarf had provided his means of rescue. Having taken in the situation and realized that, apart from the dwarf and two tethered horses, he was alone and apparently safe, Accolon now regretted his harsh words. 'Yet I must thank you for helping me escape. May I know your name so that I may thank you properly.'

'I am Darker-than-Night and Solid-as-Rock,' came the response in a voice that had suddenly taken on a tone of solemnity, 'and so I am called Calednos.'

'Then, may I thank you, Calednos. You have probably saved my life.'

'Do not thank me, thank my master, Sir Ontzlake. It was he who saw you fall over the cliff from his castle across the bay.'

Calednos pointed out across the misty sea, but Accolon could see nothing.

'The mist has now risen,' said the dwarf, 'but not an hour ago it was a bright sunny morning. Sir Ontzlake watched you walking, as if in a dream, straight over the cliff. Luckily the ledge broke your fall. He sent me hither to fetch you.'

Accolon decided he must trust the dwarf. He dropped the rope and the dwarf gathered it together and tied it over the saddle of his pony. He jumped up on to the pony's back and led the other horse over to Accolon.

'I still do not know how you knew my name,' said Accolon, as he mounted the horse.

'All will be revealed,' was all the dwarf would say.

With Calednos leading the way, the two followed the curve of the cliff. Gradually Accolon became aware of a vast edifice rising out of the mist, a castle clinging to the very face of the rocks. The path dropped into a narrow defile between the rocks and this led into a tunnel under the castle. Deep down, in a place lit only by torches fixed to the face of the rock, they dismounted, and climbed a long winding flight of steps that led them up into the castle. Accolon was taken to an antechamber where he was allowed to wash and refresh himself before he was led into a sumptuous hall, one side of which consisted entirely of windows which looked out over the sea and the precipitous cliffs. The sun had now risen high in the sky and was burning away the mists. Through the windows Accolon could see the curve of the cliffs and the spot where he had fallen. He was studying the view when he heard a voice behind him.

'Welcome, Sir Accolon.'

He turned to see a large man with broad muscular shoulders and a red, jovial smiling face, but who was hobbling into the room on crutches. Accolon immediately rushed to the man's aid and helped him towards a chair beside a table on which was set an array of fruits and sweetmeats, bread, and wine.

'Thank you,' puffed the man as he eased himself into the chair. 'Please, be seated and help yourself to food and wine. As Calednos probably told you, I am Sir Ontzlake.'

'Indeed, Sir Ontzlake, and it is you I must thank for saving my life.'

Ontzlake waved his hand as if at a trifle.

'What else should I do – let you dangle on that ledge all day? As I rose this morning and looked from my chamber window I saw you emerging from the woods and march resolutely towards the cliffs. You walked straight and determined, as if in a dream, and did not stop till you went straight over. It was a miracle that the ledge broke your fall . . .'

He hesitated and mused over what he just said. 'Or maybe no miracle at all.'

'What do you mean, Sir Ontzlake?' asked Accolon as he helped himself to some bread, cheese and grapes.

'You may wonder how I know your name,' responded Sir Ontzlake, 'and, for that matter, why I am so sorely wounded.'

Ontzlake settled himself more comfortably in his chair and sipped some wine as Accolon looked on expectantly. The elder knight frowned as he thought for a moment and then looked across at Accolon.

'For years my brother, Damas, and I have fought. Damas is a lazy, evil-minded man who has hated me ever since our father died and I inherited all the wealth. My father proclaimed that Damas would gain his portion of his inheritance only when I am defeated by a knight of good heart.

'Every month Damas sends a knight against me. He captures unwary knights and holds them in his castle over the way, but all those who are good of heart refuse to fight against me. They regard me as of good heart myself, and, even if I say so myself, I do have a reputation in this area for my good works in helping the poor and needy. Instead he sends his blackguards to do their worst, but these men are weaklings and easily disposed of. I dislike fighting them, and often pay the men to go away and return to their homelands.

'Last month, however, a knight appeared who claimed he was of good heart. He never gave his name but called himself the Knight of the Golden Fountain. He was the strongest opponent I have ever fought and he near bested me. His lance pierced my thigh, hence this wound. At that he laughed and, rather than kill me, he simply said, "My work is done," and rode away.

'Calednos did what he could to help me, but he needed to seek aid. The next day Calednos returned with a nun who claimed she came from the Convent of the Virgins of Peace. She administered unguents and gave me foul-tasting medicines, all of which seem to have worked. I am healing, but am far from fit and am unable to face this month's challenger.'

Sir Ontzlake paused and took another sip of wine, shifting himself again in his chair to ease the discomfort. Accolon waited for him to continue, knowing that a revelation was about to be made.

'The nun revisited me on several occasions to change my dressings and administer tonics. The last time was yesterday. She said that that would be her last visit and that she had a message for me. The message was that Sir Damas now had his knight of good heart who would fight me on the next new moon, which is tomorrow. Since I was still unfit, a champion could fight on my behalf.'

Ontzlake's gaze settled upon Accolon, who held a glass of wine partway to his mouth, frozen in mid-motion as he awaited the next words.

'She told me that I would find this champion the next day. That I would rescue him from yonder cliff, and that his name would be Accolon.'

He paused, but he clearly had not finished. As Accolon placed his glass of wine back on the table, Ontzlake reached down to a side table and picked up an object wrapped in fur.

'The nun also bade me to give you this, and to say that it is a gift from Morgan.'

Accolon took the object as it was handed to him. He folded back the fur wrappings and, with a sharp intake of breath, gazed upon the jewelled wonder within. There, safely sheathed within its scabbard, was Arthur's sword, Caliburn.

*

Vivian was unsettled. It was not unusual for Arthur to be away for several days on a hunting trip, but if he was going to be delayed for a prolonged period he usually sent a messenger. As the day wore on, Vivian sensed something was wrong. She sent for Merlin, but he was away. She tried to find him with her mind, but he was clearly engaged in distant and demanding work, for she could not find him. But as her mind touched the distant miles she did briefly touch the mind of Morgan. Morgan closed her defences instantly, but in that moment Vivian knew that Arthur was in trouble. She had no idea where, but the moment's vision had shown a dark dank dungeon, and she heard the name Damas.

Vivian ran from her chamber and out into the main courtyard where several knights were training, and teaching their squires.

'King Arthur is in trouble,' she cried. 'Who will help me?'

The first to turn was Sir Bors. 'What is the trouble, my lady?'

'There is no time to explain. I sense that our lord Arthur is in trouble. I do not know where, but does the name Damas mean anything?'

'It certainly does,' said Sir Breunor, who had joined Bors and Vivian. 'His castle is at least a day's ride from here. He is a violent man who is forever recruiting knights to fight his brother, because he's too much of a coward to fight him himself.'

'I believe he may have captured Arthur and is holding him prisoner in his dungeons.'

The knights asked no more questions. They called for

their squires to ready their horses and within minutes Bors, Breunor and Vivian were heading westward across the great Plain of Camelot.

Arthur had awoken with a thick head and found himself in near total darkness. It was only as his eyes grew accustomed to the dark that he perceived faint glimmers of light from the frame of a door and a few ventilation shafts in the roof. He was also aware of muttered whisperings nearby. As he moved, these whispers stopped, and he felt hands around his arms and shoulders helping him to rise.

'Welcome to the depths of despair, my friend,' said a voice.

'Where are we?'

'You are in the dungeons of the castle of Sir Damas, the vilest knight in Christendom.'

Arthur wondered why he had not heard of him if he really were that vile. Part of his mind was still puzzling over how he had arrived here from the fountain of light in the forest. He raised himself and sat on what he imagined must be a bench next to his fellow prisoner.

'Thank you, sir,' he said. 'And who is it that I thank?'

'Once I was called Sir Golygus, because of my handsome mien, but it has been years since I saw my face and I fear the name is no longer true.'

'Years?' prompted Arthur.

'Years beyond counting. Some say it has been seven years, but I believe that was before they stopped counting. Who knows how long we have festered here?'

'Why are we here?'

Had there been enough light, Arthur would have seen an expression of surprise upon the face of Golygus.

'Who is it who does not know of the dungeons of Sir Damas?'

Arthur was unsure whether to reveal his identity, but in the silence before his response there was a scratching of flint and one of the prisoners lit a small piece of cloth and held it close to Arthur's face.

'My lord Arthur. I thought I knew the voice, but I did not dare believe.'

There was consternation all round before the prisoners paid homage to their king. Then Golygus told Arthur of the dispute between Sir Damas and his brother Ontzlake, the same story as Ontzlake was at that moment telling Accolon. Arthur discovered that twenty knights were held in this prison. There they would stay unless they agreed to fight Damas's brother, and all of them refused.

'If this Sir Ontzlake is righteous and a man of his word, would he not release you without a fight?' asked Arthur.

'That he may,' replied Golygus, 'but Damas is such a false and vile knight that never could we stoop so low as to fight on his behalf.'

'You are good Christian men,' Arthur replied.

At that point, just as Arthur was about to make a proposition, there was a rattling of keys at the door and in stepped a young lady flanked on both sides by guards. She approached Arthur, but paid him no homage.

'You are to fight on behalf of my master, the lord of this castle.'

'And what if I do not?' replied Arthur.

'Then you will stay here until you die.'

Arthur had no fear in battle, especially with his sword Caliburn and its scabbard. His hand went involuntarily to his side and for the first time he realized that the sword and its sheath were missing. The damosel noticed the movement.

'Do not concern yourself. Your sword is stored safely in the armoury. You would not expect to be imprisoned complete with a weapon.'

Arthur had to regain his sword.

'My lady, tell your master that I will fight on his behalf and, if I win, all of the knights in this dungeon shall be freed.'

'Agreed.'

Arthur was surprised that this young girl could make such an agreement on her lord's behalf, but he accepted this as his opportunity to leave the dungeon.

'Then take me to your master.'

The girl led Arthur out from the dungeon. As they left Arthur paused and spoke to Golygus. 'Be brave. Soon you shall all be free.'

'But at what cost?' asked Golygus. 'If you defeat Ontzlake, you will be killing a gracious lord and raising his villainous brother to his place.'

'That will not happen in my kingdom,' replied Arthur defiantly. He turned and accompanied the girl out of the dungeon depths. As they emerged into the lighter corridors, Arthur believed the girl looked familiar.

'Have I not seen you at my court at Camelot?' he enquired.

'No, I have never been there,' the girl responded. 'I serve only my lord, Sir Damas.'

Arthur frowned, but believed her. Had his memory

served him better, he would have remembered the girl as one of the maidservants of Morgan Le Fay.

Arthur was taken through the castle to the great hall where Damas sat as if lord of his own kingdom. A large, long table was full of wine and food, whilst one wall was lined with tapestries depicting battles and adventures which were more in the dreams of Damas than his memory. Arthur was dressed in his hunting clothes and not in the fineries of his kingship, but his bearing and presence was still that of a king. Although Damas did not recognize him, or chose not to, he nevertheless recognized Arthur's character and strength and knew that this was no ordinary knight. It was evident the moment he set eyes on Arthur that here was a likely victor who would allow him to gain his rightful inheritance.

Damas proffered Arthur a seat and waved a hand at a servant to pour Arthur some wine.

'You are prepared to fight my brother and regain my inheritance?' Damas said, with no introduction.

'Only on the condition that all of the knights in your dungeons are released, a condition already agreed by your maidservant.'

Damas shifted a little uneasily in his chair and his eyes flickered towards the girl who stood behind Arthur towards the main doorway. Arthur turned to look at her and noticed the look of imperious insolence on her face. Here was a girl who served another master entirely and believed herself above her station. Arthur began to wonder whether Damas was himself a pawn in a game. If so, what did that make Arthur himself? Not for the first time, Arthur wished that Merlin was there to advise him. He did not like matters magical and mystical. He liked the solid reality of battle and the feel of steel in his hand. His thoughts came back immediately to his sword.

'If I am to be your champion,' Arthur remarked, 'you shall return to me my sword.'

'Of course, you shall have that tomorrow when the fight will take place. Today you must prepare yourself, practise, bathe, eat, and pray to God.'

So it was that on dawn of the next day Arthur rose and prepared for battle. Damas provided him with a fine suit of clothes, chainmail and armour, and Arthur was delighted to find his own blue-black stallion available. He had pondered during the previous day about his circumstances and how he came to be at the castle of Sir Damas, but no one had been prepared to answer. He could only conjecture that the Castle in the Forest had been a glamour devised by a wizard or enchantress of Sir Damas, though he had neither seen nor heard anything of this wizard. His thoughts, inevitably, turned to Morgan and he began to wonder whether this whole enterprise was another of her schemes.

As he mounted his horse, so the maidservant appeared and presented Arthur with his sword and scabbard. He was delighted to see Caliburn again. As he took the sword he frowned slightly because it felt lighter than normal. He pulled the sword from its sheath and studied it, but he could see nothing wrong. This looked every inch his sword. He flexed the blade through the air with a few trial strokes and felt satisfied.

By now Sir Damas and a retinue of knights were ready and Arthur followed them through the gates and out on to the road that would take them through the woods to the castle of Sir Ontzlake. The battle would be staged in the jousting field before the castle. At the same time, Sir Accolon was being dressed and attired, and he left Castle Ontzlake with his lord and knights. The forces of the two brothers arranged themselves on the north and south sides of the field, but Damas and Ontzlake seated themselves in chairs on a small rise on the field's western side. Arthur and Accolon jogged their steeds out into the battleground. With their visors down and wearing new sets of clothes, neither recognized the other. Nor did Arthur notice that the scabbard worn at Accolon's side looked exactly like his own.

First they couched their lances and awaited the signal to commence. The tourney master held his banner aloft and, at the signal from Sir Damas, brought it swiftly down. Accolon and Arthur spurred their horses to a trot and then a canter. The field was a furlong in width, enough for the horses to reach a fast but not a full gallop. Arthur had long learned that it was not speed but the accuracy of the spear that mattered. At full gallop it was impossible to hold the lance steady. The two great horses thundered towards each other and at the centre of the field the lances struck each shield at exactly the same moment, both precisely at the centre. Both knights fell back and were unhorsed, but both rose together and drew their swords. Accolon rushed forward first with a controlled ferocity, bringing his sword down and across with a sequence of powerful strokes. Arthur was driven immediately on to the defensive and was alarmed at the strength and accuracy of his opponent, whose sword seemed almost alive, whilst Arthur's own sword felt like cold iron in his hands. There was a sudden echoing blow to his head and Arthur felt blood trickling down his brow. Within seconds there was another blow to his shoulder where the mail was cut and blood seeped through. Although Arthur parried, and through sheer bodily strength succeeded in driving his opponent back, it was only a temporary reprieve. Arthur's physical strength may have been greater than Accolon's, but Accolon had a greater power on his side. They had been battling for less than five minutes when Arthur found himself weakening and Accolon was driving his advantage home.

Concentrating on his own survival Arthur was not aware that at that moment two other horses were galloping at full speed towards the field. Sir Bors let Vivian climb down from his horse, and then he and Sir Breunor made to enter the field to save their king, but the knights of both Sir Damas and Sir Ontzlake closed ranks and held them at bay. Vivian, however, rushed to a small rise of land near where Damas and Ontzlake sat and looked in horror upon the field. Her mind probed those of the men so she knew instantly that it was Accolon fighting Arthur and she knew that Arthur was sorely wounded and near to fainting. It was only then that she perceived the glamour about Arthur's sword and realized that it was not Caliburn. Arthur was lying prostrate on the ground using his shield to defend himself from the deadly rain of blows that came from Accolon wielding the real Caliburn. His own sword was useless and even as Vivian watched, one of Accolon's strokes shattered it.

Accolon was but a moment from victory. In the true spirit of chivalry he stood back from Arthur and spoke.

'Sir Knight, you are bested and cannot win. Your

weapon is shattered and the field runs with your blood. I do not wish to kill you. Will you yield?'

'Never,' replied Arthur. 'I have promised to fight till my last breath, and will die honourably. If you kill me weaponless, that will be your shame.'

Accolon advanced again, raising Caliburn for the death blow. In that second Vivian sent an enchantment directed at Accolon. For a brief moment a cramp seized Accolon's arm and loosened his grip on Caliburn so that as it struck Arthur's shield the sword spun from his grasp. Those watching all would later swear that the sword turned in the air and its hilt came down landing squarely in Arthur's hand. As he gripped it Arthur felt an energy surge through him and he realized that this was his true Caliburn. He knew that he had been tricked. Despite his wounds, he now forced himself to stand and pressed his advantage against Accolon. With one resounding blow Arthur struck Accolon across the helm and the knight buckled and fell. Arthur stood above the knight with his sword at Accolon's throat.

'Now you lie weaponless, but as you showed no shame, neither shall I. Before I kill you, tell me who you are.'

'My name is Accolon of Gaul, and I am a Knight of the Round Table.'

A visible shock ran through Arthur.

'Accolon, my friend. It is I, Arthur.'

He raised his visor and knelt beside Accolon, easing open that knight's visor. Accolon's head was sorely wounded and he was near to death.

'We have been bewitched, Sir Accolon. There has been trickery here, and you shall be avenged.'

He stood and called to Damas for help and was surprised to see Vivian running on to the field. Was it his own weakness through loss of blood or did he see another ghostly shape resembling Morgan, who came and knelt over Accolon as Vivian came and tended Arthur? Arthur would not yet give in to her tender care. First he commanded that she help him towards where Damas and Ontzlake sat.

As Arthur stood before Damas, the knight drew himself full and haughty in his seat, unaware of the pronouncement Arthur was about to make.

'Damas,' Arthur began, 'you are a proud and villainous knight. Even though I fought as your champion, I take no pride in that, but take pride only in that my victory shall see the release of those honourable knights whom you have kept prisoner. Through your treachery, you also kept me prisoner, your lord and king.'

The shock across Damas's face was clearly visible. Through Morgan's enchantments, he had had no idea the man before him was King Arthur. He trembled and cast himself to the ground, beseeching mercy.

'Others who crossed me I might have hanged or put to the sword, but there is a more fitting penance for you. I hereby disennoble you of your knighthood. Your lands, castle, chattels and property all shall pass to your brother, Sir Ontzlake. You may remain in your castle as tenant, but for one month out of twelve you shall be cast into your own dungeon as a penance for the knights you have unlawfully imprisoned. For twenty years this shall happen until you have served penance for each and every knight you deprived of his liberty. Only then shall you regain your castle and your lands. And if ever again I hear that you have raised a hand against a fellow knight or plotted against your brother, I shall have your head.'

Arthur was weakening rapidly from the loss of blood and it required both Sir Bors and Sir Breunor to steady him.

'Sir Ontzlake, I require your assistance,' Arthur requested. 'Please let your knights bear me and Sir Accolon to a chapel where we may be healed and cared for.'

Ontzlake made arrangements at once. Vivian followed the retinue to the nearby nunnery where the nuns prepared beds for Arthur and Accolon. Alas, Accolon was too weak and died soon after arrival. Arthur, sustained by the energy from Caliburn's scabbard, which had been restored to him, responded to treatment, but the best healer was sleep. With suitable herbs and medicine, the nuns placed Arthur in a deep slumber, while Vivian prayed in the chapel for his recovery. She brought her own healing arts to bear and was delighted to see Arthur's body responding. The wounds soon began to mend while the deep sleep restored his body and soul.

On the third day Vivian was praying in the chapel when she heard the rustle of skirts. She turned to see Morgan standing behind her.

'You believe you are so clever, sister,' she spat, 'with your little tricks. Through your interference Accolon is dead.'

It was clear that despite all her aloofness she had loved Accolon and was saddened at his death. That made her all the more dangerous.

'There are a thousand more Accolons in the world,' Morgan continued. 'Do you believe you can save Arthur from all of them? One day he will meet his match, and on that day he will not have your protection. Enough of this game—'

With that she flicked her wrist at Vivian who found herself frozen to the spot, unable to move, unable even to breathe.

Morgan sailed past her and into the room where Arthur lay. Across his breast, clasped firmly in his right hand, was Caliburn. Morgan tried to prise his fingers apart, but his grip was like steel. Morgan's power, though strong, was always weaker inside a church. Her eyes settled on the scabbard which lay at his side. She unclasped the buckle and eased the scabbard free. Now she had Arthur's only protection. She hurried from the chapel and was soon riding away.

As Morgan left, so the spell upon Vivian faded. Gasping for breath she collapsed to the floor, but forced herself to rise and to check that Arthur was unharmed. Satisfying herself that Morgan had done Arthur no ill, she hurried out of the chapel to find Bors and Breunor. She told them that Morgan had stolen Arthur's scabbard and that his life depended upon its recovery. Within minutes, Bors and Breunor were on horseback and Vivian again jumped on to the saddle behind Bors.

Their mighty coursers quickly gained on Morgan's palfrey as she rode along the cliff tops where Accolon had first fallen towards the valley of the rocks. When she realized they would soon reach her Morgan stopped and turned to face them.

'You shall witness Arthur's death warrant,' she cried, and with that she hurled the scabbard far out over the cliffs. It arced through the sky and then, because of its weight of gold and jewels, it plummeted towards the sea and sank instantly into the deep and turbulent waters.

Then Morgan spurred on her horse and galloped towards the valley of rocks. Although Bors and Breunor gained on her they soon lost sight of her amongst the rocks. Vivian searched for her mind, but could not trace her. She knew that Morgan had shape-changed both herself and her horse into an outcrop of rocks, and so expert was Morgan at this deception that even Vivian could not see any evidence of the glamour.

At length Bors and Breunor ceased their searches and returned to the chapel where they were greeted by a revived and much restored Arthur. But it was a sad Arthur who the next day returned with Vivian and his knights to Camelot. Vivian may have saved Arthur this time, but Morgan had sown yet another seed of fate.

5. The Stones of Broceliande

Summer, and the deep woods of Broceliande. Oak and birch, miles beyond miles, murmurous with doves and bees, swift with soft breezes from the distant sea, blue and green – everywhere, blue and green. Merlin and Vivian, side by side under a vast benevolent beech tree, rested on deep drifts of beech-leaves, drowsily content.

'Lovely place,' sighed Merlin. 'I wish I could stay here for ever.'

Vivian reached out a hand to touch him.

'Don't say it. Some Power might hear you and grant your wish.'

'So?' He raised himself on his elbow, smiling. 'But why not? I need a rest. So long as you were with me, of course.'

They had come to Broceliande to attend the funeral of Merlin's old master, Blaise the Arch-Magician. Merlin and Vivian and their lovely daughter, Blaisine, now seventeen years old, had joined the long line of white-robed Druids that wound slowly up and down the long straight lines of mysterious stones, the Place of the Magicians. Vivian, at Merlin's recommendation, had been invested with the green robe of an Ovate, and the young Blaisine had worn the blue robe of a novice magician, with her raven-dark hair bare. They had all, those grave and dedicated men and women, greeted the mother and daughter as new and welcome companions among them. All spoke the Celtic tongue, though with strange differences according to the places from whence they came, for the magicians had come from all over Gaul, from Scotland and Eire, and from the cold northern countries, to honour Blaise, the teacher of all magicians, and to install Merlin as his successor.

Merlin's honour was great, but most of all it was great because of King Arthur. Through Merlin, Arthur had brought peace and prosperity to Britain. It was a Golden Age that Merlin had striven long and hard for. He knew that he had not bested Morgan, and that her tricks might still win the day, but for now Britain and Arthur were safe. Merlin believed it was time for him to rest.

Merlin reflected on all this as he sat with Vivian.

'I'm so tired, my dear,' he said. 'Tired and old. I know we people of the Other Place live again, from life to life, but *this* particular body is growing tired. How old am I? You don't know. I don't know. I've placed Arthur on his throne, given him his sword and his kingdom, and now I don't think he needs me any more.'

'Don't say it.' Vivian gave his shoulder a little shake. 'It's not true. Arthur needs you and will need you. There is trouble coming to him, sore trouble. Surely, you know?'

'Oh I know,' he sighed. 'Mordred, and now Lancelot. I know, but I can't prevent it.'

'Perhaps not, but there are things for you to do. How

often have you told me, Merlin, that fate must take its course, but men have their own choice as to how they shall take it, and how others shall take it. You have work to do for the sake of those not yet born. I, also, can see ahead.'

'Two prophets,' he said smiling. 'And neither sees the same road as the other, though perhaps both see the same end. Well, well, let it be so. I'll go back to Camelot soon, when I have rested. Meantime, it is very pleasant here.'

'So it is,' she agreed, 'and it's time I fetched our meal. I think Blaisine is walking in the woods with young Nentres.'

'Nentres, yes, a good lad. She might do worse, though she's young yet. Yes, time to eat. Shall we go back?'

'No, you stay here and sleep a little longer. I'll fetch it from the cottage. I shan't be long.'

She stepped away through the green on her way to the little forest lodge where they had taken up their quarters for the summer. She looked back once.

'He's asleep already,' she said to herself. 'Perhaps I ought to put a circle of protection around him, but who would harm him here?'

Merlin had been asleep some time when he woke and saw Vivian standing over him.

'I've brought the basket,' she said, 'but it's too hot to stay out here. Let's find a cooler place. I know, let's go to the Old Mound. It should be cool there.'

Merlin rose to his feet. The sun was certainly blazing, and the thought of the cool stone cell seemed attractive.

'This way, then,' he said, and led the way. It was about half-a-mile, but the wood changed as they went. The translucent beeches gave way to tall pines, sweetly giving off their gummy scent in the sun, and then to dark yews. Embowered in their midst was the great barrow, called the Old Mound by some and the King's Chamber by others. The yews were shady, but the air was still hot and oppressive. Vivian set the basket down and leaned against the barrow.

'Let's go inside,' she said. 'It's so hot out here, I can't bear it.'

'Why go inside, my dear? It's no sort of place to eat our meal. Let us stay out here.'

'No, no, it's too hot. Merlin, please take me inside. I feel I'm going to faint.'

'My dear, the door opens only by magic, you know.'

'Of course I know.' Her tone was querulous, but weak. Certainly she was suffering in the heat – it was seldom she was so peevish. Merlin became anxious for her. 'I know it works by magic, but I don't know the words. *You* know them. Now, for heaven's sake, use the magic and let us get out of this glare. What's the use of being a magician . . .'

'All right, my dear, all right,' Merlin responded, unused to this manner, and wondering whether Vivian had a touch of the sun. He stepped up to the door and spoke two words, loudly and clearly. Then he placed his shoulder against the door stone and pushed. It swung round on a pivot, revealing the vault inside.

It was not altogether dark. Of the three chambers into which the barrow's interior was divided, the earth had fallen away from the side of one, and the stone wall had been broken open by a narrow fissure, through which a glimmer of light penetrated. Merlin supported Vivian into the chamber. The open door behind them gave a little light also, reflected round the turn of the wall. But it was a dim and stony place.

Vivian gave a sigh of relief and sank down to the floor. There was a low shelf, as for a seat, along the wall, and Merlin seated himself there. Vivian breathed deeply and then got up.

'This is so much better. It's a benign place, isn't it, Merlin, beautifully cool?'

'Yes, my dear. All the bones of the old kings are long since gone. But don't shut the door. If you did we couldn't open it again from the inside; it only opens from the outside, and then it wants both words, and a strong man's arm to push it.'

'And what are the words?'

Merlin paused, but then whispered them to her.

'And the shutting spell?'

'There isn't one, but if it were shut it could only be opened from the outside. Leave it till we go out.' His voice rang hollowly among the stony cells.

'It's so cool and I feel so much better,' she said. 'I'll go and fetch the basket and we'll eat here.'

She stood up and took two steps round the corner to where the three cells joined the passage, and then out through the door. Merlin heard her footsteps and then, not believing what he heard, the swing of the heavy stone, and the dull bang as it closed. He saw the reflected light from the doorway disappear. He ran to the entrance. The door was shut fast.

'Vivian,' he called, repeating her name several times.

From the other side of the cell he heard a laugh. He

groped his way back to the fissure through which the gleam of light came. It was the length of the wall, but scarcely a finger's width wide. Through it he could glimpse Vivian moving backward and forward before it, and he could hear her voice.

'So there you are, dear Merlin. I've beaten you now. You're trapped and you know it. There you shall stay. No one will ever find you.'

He almost fainted. Propping himself against the wall by the crack, he cried, 'Vivian, Vivian, my love. Is this a jest? For God's sake, let me out.'

'This is no jest,' she mocked from the daylight world. 'You'll stay there till you die and your body rots. Your ghostly body can escape, we know that, but what use will that be to Arthur? You can do nothing more in this world. Clever old Merlin is finished.' And she broke into a cackle of laughter.

'Are you mad, or am I? Vivian, this is so unlike you. What is it? What have I done?'

'What have you done?' Through the crack he could see her dancing on the pine needles. 'What have you done?' She now spat out the words. 'You have wearied me over the years. Did you think I loved you? I'm tired of you, you old fool. Now you can rot there in the darkness.'

Merlin slipped to the ground and lay there, crouched, his hands over his eyes, while his whole world shattered around him in horror, grief and despair. Half-smothered cries broke from him in the darkness.

'Vivian, Vivian, after all these years. We were so happy together. I thought you loved me. You were the truest, most loving wife a man ever had. Was it all deceit? I would as soon have doubted God as doubted you. And now it's gone. I'm lost. What a fool I must have been. I just do not understand. Oh God, let me die quickly . . .'

His tormentor might have left him to die there in utter despair, but she could not resist the pleasure of tormenting him, of bragging to him. He must see her cleverness.

'Look at me again, Merlin,' she said.

'Go away and leave me. I have come to an end.'

'No, but look just once more. You will be astonished.'

Something in the tone of her voice was different. He lifted his head and looked through the crack. Golden sandals – Vivian never wore golden sandals. White-robed, gleeful, exulting, it was Morgan who stood beyond.

'Oh yes, Merlin, my arch-mage, my arch-Enemy. I fooled you, didn't I? How could you forget how clever we were at shape-changing – and I was always the best of all. Now I have won the last game. Didn't I take Vivian's shape well? Poor Vivian. She lies by the cottage with my long knife through her heart.'

Tears started from Merlin's eyes and streamed down his face – tears both of relief and of devastating pain.

'Oh Vivian, my true, my loving wife. You never betrayed me. Vivian, you are still mine. Morgan, you creature of evil – you cannot kill her spirit any more than you can kill mine. Our spirits will fly away together into the place of bliss and the gardens of the West.'

'Yes, oh yes, and leave Britain to me and my people! You know, Merlin, what will become of your Arthur, and his Guinevere, and his knights of the Round Table, and his kingdom of Britain. Mine. Your body won't get out of there, and Vivian's ghost-body can't get you out, not even if you taught her the words.'

'There's Blaisine,' he insisted, and then wished he had not uttered her name for fear of Morgan's retribution.

'Your Blaisine lies asleep in the woods in the arms of young Nentres. I have placed a strong spell upon them, the spell of love. They will not wake from their charmed sleep for many days. You will have parched with drought by then. Your Vivian's ghost will not be able to feed you, only to invite you to leave your body. Indeed, the sooner you do, the less you will suffer. Sleep well and long, my dear Merlin, until our next meeting in Destiny's pathway. I'll away to see what can be done in Camelot.'

And she was gone from the narrow slip of light leaving Merlin alone.

Earlier that same morning, Blaisine and Nentres, straying in the woods, enjoying the glory of high summer, saw Vivian coming towards them, radiant and tripping over the beech-leaves. Blaisine noticed, but without more than slight curiosity, that her mother had borrowed her aunt's gold sandals.

'Children, children,' Vivian sang out. 'A lovely day for you, a blessed augury. Children, I have been studying the stars and they say that today, today as ever is, must be your wedding day. Come, your bridal is all set for you. Today, children.'

They looked at one another and then at her, in surprise.

'But Mother – what about the King and the Queen? What about all our friends and relatives? What of Nentres's kin? What of Father?'

'Your father will be here in his own time, darling,' she said. 'As for our kinsfolk, and the King and Queen, there will be a more stately celebration when we return to

Camelot. But the stars say that we must take the day, now, and even the hour is important. I have a priest here. He is a hermit, and has a shrine that is a holy place. Come, come, my darlings.'

'But how shall I be dressed, Mother?'

'By magic, my dear. Nentres, you have known all along that we are all magicians. You don't object to marrying into a magician's family?' She smiled affectionately on him.

'Shall we go back to the cottage?' asked Blaisine, turning in its direction.

'No, no, I don't want you to go back to the cottage yet. There is no need.' Vivian drew both hands smoothly down Blaisine, from her head to her feet, and there stood Blaisine in glimmering pale green, like the beech-leaves, girdled with silver and crowned with a braid of the white-flowered convolvulus, over a veil like the mist of morning. She gasped with delight. Nentres, by her side, was in a long tunic of white brocade, with a wide chain round his neck of silver and crystals.

'But this is glamour,' said Blaisine.

'The glamour is only the adornment, my darling, to do you honour and give you pleasure.'

A few steps through the woodland led them to a glade which their rambles through the woods had never showed them before. In the glade was a small chapel of white stone, where a reverend old hermit was gently ringing a soft-sounding bell. Inside was an altar, with candles, though there did not seem to be any cross. Perhaps it was hidden by the great sheaf of flowers on the altar. There the bride and bridegroom, and the bride's mother, paced slowly in and stood before the hermit. Blaisine looked round for Merlin, who should have led her in on his arm to give her to Nentres, but he was not there, and the hermit did not wait for him. In something of a daze the two repeated the holy vows, and Nentres took his own ring from his finger and placed it on Blaisine's.

When the rite was over Vivian led them through a door at the back of the chapel, and there was a pavilion, with a feast set out – no guests but themselves, but a sumptuous repast. They ate and drank, hardly knowing what they did – it was all so surprising. And then it seemed to be a starry night, and Vivian led them into another pavilion where there was a wide bed, richly draped and soft. With her own hands she undressed the bride, laid her in the bed and closed the curtains over them both. Soft music breathed over the lovers from unseen musicians. Then the lady in the golden sandals sped softly away. Morgan, still in the shape of Vivian, went through the woods to Merlin . . .

Later, she came past the stone chamber a second time and listened at the crack. From inside she could hear deep, broken sobbing groans. She took the dark mantle which she was wearing and flung it over the stones so that it covered the crack. Now there would be no light at all within, and no air.

6. The Door Without a Key

Merlin lay in the dark for longer than he could reckon. There was no light now, not even the little glimmer from the crack which had let in first the sunset colours and then the moonlight. Nor was there the slender thread of fresh air, like the draught through a keyhole, to which he had set his lips to breathe. The panic fear of suffocation began to grip him. He tore his clothes away from his neck. Panting, he tried to control himself. He must not start to struggle. That was no good. He was to die anyhow, whatever he did. He wished it would be soon. He was parched with thirst. He remonstrated with himself. *You so-called magician, can't you get yourself out of this? Use your arts. Yes, but to work magic you must have a clear head, and energy of mind, spirit and body.*

But he had no energy. It was all gone and he was too weak to counter the malicious will that he could feel opposing him. He could only see what Morgan wanted him to see, the fate of his beloved Britain, Morgan triumphant, the power around the Round Table turned to lawlessness and selfish violence. No God, no Gospel, no churches. One worship only, that of the great deceiver,

Morgan. And Arthur, drawn all too easily into the ways of destruction, ravaging Britain and damning his own soul. At the thought great sobs wrenched his breast, but he could draw no air into his labouring lungs. Oh God in heaven! he thought. Let me die quickly!

Blaisine stirred slowly from the blissful sleep of love. Someone was calling her. *Blaisine . . . Blaisine . . .* She put a groping hand out towards her bridegroom. 'Darling, did you call?' There was no reply.

Dimly she perceived that she was lying not on a feather bed, but on beech-leaves, and that over her was no canopy, but a tracery of boughs. All was sweet and still, and such a heavy drowsiness lay upon her that she could not rouse herself. Perhaps she was still dreaming? She slept again.

She heard it again, louder now. *Blaisine, Blaisine. It is I, your mother. Your mother, Blaisine.* With heavy eyes still shut she listened, her body taut with attention. Then she thought she heard her mother's voice speak a special word that she recognized from the magic that Vivian had long ago taught her, a word that had been a secret between them. Startled, she opened her eyes and lifted herself on her elbow. Nentres was by her side, but he was still deeply asleep. She looked round for her mother, but saw no one.

The voice spoke again.

This is your mother, Blaisine. Shut your eyes, but keep awake and listen to me.

Blaisine sank bank on the moss pillow behind her, shut her eyes, and placed her hands as Vivian had taught her for meditation. The voice spoke as if clearly beside her.

Blaisine, your father is in great danger. Get up at once, wake Nentres, go, the both of you, to the Old Mound, the King's Chamber. Your father is trapped under the stone. Morgan has done this. Go at once or you will be too late. Don't go back to the cottage. Go to the Mound at once, at once!

She opened her eyes again. She had thought it must be morning, but the sun was setting. She shook Nentres, who murmured a sleepy endearment and turned to sleep again. She shook him harder.

'Nentres, wake up. Father is in danger.'

'Danger?' The word got through his sleep. He opened his eyes. 'Beloved, what's the matter? What's happened? Where are we? This isn't where we—'

'No matter. Don't stop to ask. Come quickly.'

'I'll come, but where's my sword? And how did you know all this?'

'My mother, the real one, not Morgan, called to me in spirit. Now come, oh come quickly, or we may be too late.'

Merlin lay in the exhausted air, stretched on the stone bench, only his chest twitching from moment to moment with a convulsive spasm. A drowsiness was coming over him, and he welcomed it.

Then, amazingly, there was a light, bluish and phosphorescent, and Vivian herself walked clear through the stone wall. No golden sandals. Her feet were bare.

'Oh Merlin, my love,' she cried. 'It is I, really myself, not Morgan.' She knelt by him and spoke into his ear a lovers' secret known only to those two. He knew that this was no glamour, but his true Vivian, but when he reached out to clasp her, there was nothing there.

'Are you out of the body?' he croaked through his parched lips.

'Yes, my love. My body lies in the orchard by the cottage, with Morgan's knife through my heart. I am free to go now.'

'Then let us go together, my dear. I shall be glad to be rid of this—'

'No, dear Merlin, not yet. I came here to keep you in body a while longer. You have much to do yet.'

'Oh, blessed God, must I?' His breath rasped like a wind over dead leaves. 'Let me go, just let me go. I am worn out.'

'No, dear. Stay in the body.'

She placed her weightless spirit arms on his shoulders and pressed him down. The ghost-shape that was trying to rise and escape from his body was held there, though his earthly body suffered and longed to give up the ghost.

'Let me go,' he urged.

'No, my darling husband, no. If you leave your body now, you'll never get back again. You have to live to help the world, and Arthur. And to help one that is yet to be born. My dear, I know you suffer.' She released his shoulders and held out her hands before him like a cup. To his eyes they seemed to become a cup filled with liquid light. He drank from it – water, sweet wine, honey, the fresh morning air, all were in that draught. It revived him a little, his body as well as his protesting spirit. He sank back and rested for the moment.

'Tell me the opening spell,' she said.

He repeated the words, saying, 'Can you use it now to get me out of here?'

'No, my dear, you know I can't. I may say it, but my ghost-body cannot move the stone, only an earthly body can do that. But Blaisine and her knight Nentres are coming. Hold up, my dear, and keep the life in your poor body a little longer.'

'How long, Vivian? I am tired of struggling. Let me sleep and suffer no more.'

'No!' she almost shrieked. 'You must not sleep, you shall not. That is not sleep but death. Keep awake, for me, and for the world.'

Her invisible bosom and arms cradled Merlin, rocked him and shook him, and breathed into him the thin and tremulous life of the spirit.

The dark was rapidly falling as Blaisine and Nentres plunged into the woods. There was a path, which Blaisine knew would lead to the Old Mound, though it twisted about and broke and hid. In the faint light of a half-moon they followed it. Suddenly, out of the ground before them, with a hissing noise, rose up a white thing like a monstrous mushroom, springing from the dead leaves – a pale, tall, obscene column. They halted in their tracks as the thing confronted them. It shone with a baleful light, a glow of rottenness. The head of it seemed to peer round at them before it broke and expanded, dissolved into white mist, grew thick again, and there stood Morgan, eyes blazing, arms outstretched.

'Go back,' she commanded them. 'Go back to the blissful sleep I gave you, you fools. Why must you wake to sorrow?'

'Let us pass, aunt Morgan. We must go on.'

'No, my dear niece. Don't be in such a hurry. Go back

to your cottage and see what has happened to your mother.'

Nentres made as to turn and run back, but Blaisine held his arm.

'No, Nentres, we can do nothing there. My father needs us more.'

'Why you obstinate child,' said the white apparition, 'will you not run to your mother's help?'

'My father's need is greater,' said Blaisine. 'I know where my mother is, and you have killed her. Out of the way, you murderer.'

'You are both unarmed,' mocked Morgan. 'I saw to that. Who takes anything of metal into the bridal bed? There is nothing you can do.'

'I can do this,' said Nentres, between clenched teeth, and with his bare hands he sprang straight at Morgan's throat.

Morgan was caught unprepared, too wrapped up in her mockery of the children and her belief in her mastery of the situation. She fell backward to the ground with Nentres's hands still fastened to her throat. Morgan struggled and thrashed, and her hands were free.

'Take care!' cried Blaisine. 'She has a dagger!'

Blaisine knelt by the side of the others as they struggled and grasped the long knife that was almost at Nentres's breast. Standing erect she held the dagger by its point, making a cross of it. In the hands of some this would have availed little against Morgan's great evil power, but a passion of faith and devotion shot through Blaisine's innocent and pure heart like a lightning flash, and blazed through the steel cross into Morgan's eyes. Nentres felt the witch-woman's struggles fail and her limbs fall inert.

'Now, quick,' cried Blaisine, 'bind her before she recovers. Use your girdle and mine. I'll put power on them.' The girdles, as Nentres bound them round Morgan's hands and ankles, swelled and toughened, and clung like snakes. 'Let these hold,' Blaisine intoned in the voice of a chanter, while she still held the dagger as a cross, 'in the Name of the Father, and of the Son and of the Holy Ghost. Amen.'

The vanquished woman spoke from the ground. 'Let me go, or I'll put a curse on you.'

'Not for any curse you can utter,' said Blaisine. 'Come, Nentres, we must hurry.'

'Then my curse go with you,' came Morgan's tormented voice and she struggled against the charmed bonds. 'Your child, Blaisine, and yours, Nentres, your child shall never know its parents.'*

'Don't look back,' cried Blaisine to Nentres, who had hesitated. 'Not once; leave her there. Come on, come on,' and they hastened away into the dark woods, Blaisine still holding the dagger cross-wise.

Running hand-in-hand, breathless, they reached the Old Mound at last, and fell exhausted against the rocky side. No one could be seen.

'Mother! Father!' cried Blaisine. 'Are you here? Are you alive? Oh, do speak!'

No voice came from her mother but, groping, she felt a heavy mantle lying upon the stone. She flung it aside and then heard Merlin's voice, very faint.

'Say these words,' he spoke plainly though falteringly, 'and then push the stone.'

* Note: the fulfilment of this curse is told in *The Green Knight*.

Nentres set his shoulder against the rock, and Blaisine repeated the words, a loud cry, two piercing syllables. The rock swung round and the dark entrance to the barrow was revealed.

Blaisine rushed past Nentres and vanished from his sight into the cavity. He followed. There was a turn in the dark passage and then a glimmer of light. Thick filaments of ancient dust hung down from him as he went in, soft stalactites of blackness that brushed his face as he passed, shuddering. Inside the chamber a thin pencil of light lay across a group of three people, he thought, and touched their shape. Merlin lay stretched out on a bed of stone, and two women bent over him. Nentres heard Vivian's unmistakable voice saying, *Help him out of here,* but when he stooped to gather up Merlin's inert form, he could feel only Blaisine helping, no one else. They laid Merlin on the ground outside the barrow. Nentres looked round for Vivian.

'Where is your mother? I heard her voice.'

'No matter, now, Nentres. I know where she is. Shut the door of the mound.'

'But, no, if your mother is still in there?'

'She is not there. Close the door.'

So Nentres gave a thrust to the great stone and it closed with a grating thud; the echoes rang hollowly down the depths of the chamber.

Back at the cottage while Blaisine tenderly nursed Merlin back to life, Nentres searched the house and the garden. He found, in the apple orchard, the body of Vivian, stretched prone on the ground with a long knife through her back. But when he turned her over, the dead face was smiling.

7. So Passes Arthur

Moonlight, the full moon, and a windless night; there was the white light shining unearthly on the sea, and on the long mere divided from the sea by a narrow ridge of pebbles that sighed as the small waves rolled them up and drew them back.

There were no trees or shrubs along the ridge, but on the far side of the mere, beyond the pale straight reeds and the sleeping swans, were willows, fringing the bank, their long branches of straight thin leaves trailing their tips in the water. Motionless and silvery in the moonlight, they rose up like frozen fountains. And in the heart of the tallest willow, those with a certain gift of sight might have seen the shadowy shapes of Merlin and Vivian.

Shapes with no mortal substance left to them, for fifteen years had passed since Merlin's reprieve from the stone tomb of Broceliande, in spite of Morgan. Death had at last found him and he had departed from the body beside the altar of Stonehenge when he gave his life to save that of his granddaughter, the second Vivian, Blaisine's child who, indeed, never knew her parents. Sir

Gawain the Younger had, at that time, crushed Morgan into the earth when Merlin had vanquished her, but such as Morgan do not die so easily.* Seven years more had the young Gawain's willing sacrifice purchased for King Arthur, but now Arthur's time had come. In a convent in Wimborne, Ursulet, Arthur's daughter, was a child of seven, not knowing anything of what was happening in the world; and, in a moated grange in Lyonesse, a boy of five, the son of the young Gawain, dreamed of rescuing a princess.† Guinevere, a penitent in black and white robes, dwelt yet in Amesbury; Lancelot was still in far-off France. And Arthur's evil hour had come.

Far inland over the plains, corpses of men and horses lay hideously scattered, bathed in the cold light of the pitiless moon. Somewhere among them, Sir Bedivere, the last Knight of the Round Table, knelt on the ground beside Arthur, vainly trying to staunch his many wounds.

The ghost-body of Merlin and the ghost-body of Vivian clung together under the willow tree. Their limbs and bodies were like faint line drawings, delicately etched in with lines of the willow twigs. Only their eyes were brilliant. Their speech together was more like waves of thought conveyed on faint notes of music.

Merlin, is this the end?

It is the end of the Round Table, and of King Arthur's realm as we know it. Mordred's army and Arthur's army have wiped each other out. No, Mordred is not dead. He will strive again, and once again he will summon Morgan in all her power to aid him. But I shall not be there – to

* Note: these events are told in *The Green Knight*.

† Note: these events are told in *King Arthur's Daughter*.

my sorrow. Yet I think they will call me back once more before the very last time.

The very last time? Then is Arthur and all he fought for to slip away into the darkness and be forgotten?

No, never forgotten, Vivian my love. Arthur must die now, but Arthur will come again. None knows yet in what way he will come, but I know this, he will never, never be forgotten. His spirit will go on, and so shall his work, for he is Britain.

Vivian sighed and relaxed in Merlin's arms. Then she lifted her head again.

Listen, one comes through the trees. He comes to the shore – look.

The two watchers saw Sir Bedivere, his battered and grimy armour gleaming wanly in the moonlight, come alone down to the water's edge. In his hand he held Arthur's sword, the magical sword Caliburn that Vivian had taken from Shony and given to Merlin to place in the stone for Arthur to draw forth.

That sword, she murmured to Merlin, *what will he do with it?*

He ought to give it back whence it was taken.

Whence I took it, said Vivian, and shuddered through her transparent substance at the recollection. *I could not let that be returned to Old Shony.*

Then do what you must do.

Sir Bedivere looked at the sword in the moonlight, then turned aside and hid it among the branches at the water's edge, and disappeared into the dark wood.

Oh, the fool, breathed Vivian.

I think he will come back, said Merlin, his voice a vibration upon a bass string.

They waited in silence among the willow leaves. Presently they heard the footsteps again and the crunch of gravel at the water's edge, as Sir Bedivere stepped down to the water.

Nearer. No, boy, don't hesitate.

But Bedivere did hesitate, and hid the sword again, and went back into the darkness.

I think next time he will do it, said Vivian, and so saying, she stepped on to the lake's surface. Her ghost body allowed her to walk upon other planes. At the centre of the mere she allowed herself to sink into the waters.

She heard Bedivere return, walking faster and with more resolution. Now he took the sword from its hiding place, and firmly bound the rich plaited belt around its scabbard – a new one that Arthur had had made, not the original, which was back with Old Shony. Bedivere raised it high in the moonlight, whirled it round in a wide circle, hearing it scintillate and whistle in the still air. Three times he whirled it and then sent it flying out across the mere.

Vivian was ready. As the blade arced over the water she raised her arm above the lake and the sword settled firmly in her hand. Bedivere watched spellbound, aware of the glowing ghostly arm which now grasped the blade, brandished it three times, and slowly sank beneath the surface.

Bedivere turned and walked back to his dying king, as Vivian returned to Merlin.

I will keep the sword safe for Arthur, she said.

As she spoke she became aware of a movement in the mist. From the dim reaches of the mere a barge approached, soundless on the glassy water. Two rowers in black cowls that hid their faces were moving it forward with long sweeps. In the stern were two women, also black-robed, who were spreading pillows and rugs to make a couch in the barge. They woke the air with a soft, clear singing, infinitely mournful.

My two sisters, whispered Vivian. *They are getting ready to take Arthur. Will they never cease? We must stop them.*

No, you must go and join them, said Merlin. *Good and evil must balance round him, as they balanced at his birth. Morgan, evil illusion and lies; Morgause, neutral and sensual, and easily drawn to the bad; yourself, the shining good. Britain will always be balanced so. Go down, my sweetheart, for every hour that the balance is out of true, Britain is in danger.*

Vivian and Merlin clasped each other one last time, and with the tenderest of ghostly kisses, Vivian slipped away from his side. Merlin watched as Vivian silently walked across the lake to the barge. It was the end of another age and Merlin wondered when he and Vivian-Nimuë would meet again, and in what circumstances.

There came the sound of a single horse, slowly approaching the shore. Bedivere, leading his great war-horse, was carefully supporting the inert form of Arthur, slung across the saddle. Gently he lifted the limp body into the stern of the barge, and the three women arranged themselves around it. Morgause, in the middle, took the weight of the body, Morgan took his feet in her lap, and Vivian cradled his head upon her breast. Softly, in turns, and then together, they sang of the deeds of Arthur, and of his end.

To Avalon, to Avalon, to heal him of his deadly wound;
In Avalon there will be no more time or space for him.
From Avalon we will bear him to his secret refuge,
Where he shall lie among his knights till the time is come.
Deep under hollow hills he shall lie,
Each knight with his sword at his side, and his shield at his head,
Where lamps perpetual shine upon their peace,
And silence is a music meet for their requiem.

And Vivian said, *I nursed him at my breast. None of you loved him as I did.*

Morgause said, *My baby brother, so passionately I desired him.*

And Morgan said, *My noble enemy – is there not a kind of love between such?*

But Merlin, watching the barge as it moved slowly out across the water and disappeared into the mist, said, *He will come again.*

And Bedivere, on his knees by the waterside, though he could not hear Merlin, said from his own heart:

'Pray, he will come again.'